I0526962

UNLEASHED & UNCORKED

A KAT & KOA MYSTERY
BOOK 1

JULIA MERLOT

GLOBAL SHORES
PUBLISHING

This book is a work of fiction. The characters, incidents, and dialogue are drawn from the author's imagination and are not to be construed as real. Any resemblance to actual setting, events or persons, living or dead, is entirely coincidental, archetypal, a result of tapping into the collective unconscious, or a mishmash of the author's life encounters with characters real or imagined, or perhaps personality-driven composite characters; which is to say – if you think you recognize yourself or another as one of the characters, that should be construed as a result of your own projection and not the author's expressed intent. Despite having written the above disclaimer, my neighbors would like you to know that they are NOT alcoholics.

Unleashed & Uncorked. Copyright © 2025 by Julia Merlot.

All rights reserved under International and Pan-American Copyright Conventions. By payment of the required fees, you have been granted the non-exclusive, non-transferable right to access and read the text of this e-book on-screen. No part of this text may be reproduced, transmitted, downloaded, decompiled, reverse engineered, or stored in or introduced into any information storage and retrieval system, in any form or by any means, whether electronic or mechanical, now known or hereafter invented, without the express written permission of Global Shores Publishing. GlobalShoresLLC@gmail.com

EPub and Print Edition © March 2025

ISBN: 979-8-9889663-3-3

PRAISE FOR JULIA MERLOT

"A delightfully quirky mystery with just the right amount of ghostly charm and canine intelligence. If Kat and Koa don't steal your heart, the Prosecco will!"

— NEIL GAIMUTT, AUTHOR OF *GOOD BONES*

"With ghosts, murder, and an irresistibly clever dog, this book kept me entertained from start to finish. A must-read for anyone who likes their mysteries with a splash of wine and a wag of the tail!"

— GILLIAN BONE, AUTHOR OF *GONE FUR GOOD*

"An intoxicating blend of charm, suspense, and furry companions. If Legacy Lake were real, I'd move in tomorrow—ghosts and all!"

— TANA FRENCH BULLDOG, AUTHOR OF *THE SECRET HOUND*

CONTENTS

ABOUT THIS BOOK

How well do you really know your neighbors?

Kat Drexler-Morai was hoping for a quiet summer with her newly adopted Portuguese Water Dog, Koa, in a peaceful cabin on the shores of Legacy Lake. Instead, she gets murder, mayhem, and a couple of ghosts with attitude.

When a real estate mogul drops dead at a wine-tasting party, nearly everyone in Legacy Lake and Liberty Ridge has a motive—and no one has an alibi. But Kat quickly realizes the neighbors have put *her* at the top of their suspect list. Now, she has to clear her name before she's trading in her Antiques and Oddities business for an orange jumpsuit.

With a town full of quirky (and questionably innocent) neighbors, a dog who insists on sniffing out trouble, and a *very* sexy (hunka hunka burning love) ghostly houseguest, Kat soon realizes lakeside living feels less like a cozy retreat and more like starring in a murder mystery reality show.

Legacy Lake's *Driveway Detective Party* team has gathered for yet another round of "let's accuse our neighbors of murder," served with fizzy beverages and a light drizzle of suspicion.

A barkin' good read packed with mystery, mischief, and a splash of bubbly!

PEACE AND PAWSIBILITIES

I'm going to blame my cousin Maggie for all of this. Maggie, youngest daughter of my mother's sister, who used to get me into all sorts of trouble when we were kids, sweetly convinced me to move into this cozy little cabin by the lake with promises of peace, quiet, and nothing more stressful than deciding whether to drink my coffee on the deck or on the dock.

I should have known she hadn't changed and would lead me into double trouble of the adult kind. Thanks to Maggie, I anticipated living in a Hallmark movie village, falling in love with a charming local millionaire masquerading as a handyman and sipping fine wine in waterfront bistros. Instead, I've stumbled into a neighborhood filled with murderous intent and more than a few secret skeletons buried in the woods behind my house.

How did I come to rent this lakeside cabin? Long story. Predictable. I won't bore you with much but to say it's the age-old story - husband left for a younger, wealthier model. I consoled myself by focusing on my antiques and oddities business travelling almost compulsively for several years. And when business suffered after the Planetary Plandemic

Prototype followed by the shocking Recession Reality Reset, I felt spun out and longed for a stable community where I could clear my head and find my heart's center again.

So here I am, standing at the window of my cabin, with the air conditioning blasting full throttle because Maggie failed to mention that summer here is like living in Satan's dry sauna. My long, chestnut hair tied in a ponytail. My eyes squinting into the light of day. Legacy Lake stretched out before me, a giant, mirror-like puddle of should be tranquility, but long days released the endless stream of guys in fishing boats and kayakers surfing the giant waves generated by wake boats shattering the skies with big bass-thumping rap music. Hard to consider taking a swim when it felt more like bodysurfing to shore. Hard to imagine putting on my on a swimsuit!

Sure, I've done yoga and hiked enough trails to feel *moderately* in shape, but let's be honest—nobody after the age of 40 gets excited about squeezing into Spandex after years of stress-snacking piled an extra 20 pounds onto my short frame. It was time to get real and get back into shape.

Apart from the swoooosh of the air conditioner kicking on and off, the cabin was quiet, far too quiet, in that way that silence becomes a presence, edging into your personal space like an anxious guest who refuses to perch in one place and insists on following you around the kitchen. I could hear the long sigh of my own exhale as I stood at the window, looking out over the water. *Go swim, lazy butt.* I chastised myself. *Get out of your head and at least lounge on a floatie. Why have a lake house if you don't get in the water? Enjoy it before fall falls!*

Fall would be here all too soon, lurking like a shadow just out of reach, filling the space between the golden leaves that clung stubbornly to the branches. It wouldn't be long until they blew away, leaving the trees skeletal, their bare limbs reaching up toward the slate-gray sky. Winter would follow, blanketing everything in white, ice covered by snow, pressing the world into a deep hush, and here I would be, alone in this little cabin at the edge of Legacy Lake, staring at ice with no one but ghosts to keep me company.

Literally.

Ghosts of the woo-woo type. Not ghosts that arise from past memories haunting me until I die. Although I admit, I do have one or two and a few regrets. Anyone who says they don't have regrets is either a liar or has dismissed the past under the haze of drugs or dementia.

I see interactive spirits mostly. They often come to me in a dream. Once in a while, I see them running around during the day. Once they have my attention, well. Things happen. I wouldn't say I am a psychic. More of a Seer. I see with all six senses. And fortunately, I only meet an occasional guest who requests something of me. And I can say no. I often do.

But instead, I just stood there, staring at the water, spiraling into existential musings about the seasons and life, my thoughts leapfrogging one past another as if I had ADD. Now wondering whether or not I should dye my roots to match my hair – or go au natural. Au natural swimming seemed like a better idea. Best wait until after the lights go out on the lake. Clearly my brain has not slowed down a bit since I moved in a few weeks ago.

And then, out of nowhere, a thought hit me like a rogue mosquito: *This cabin is the best place to raise a puppy. You need a dog.* At first, I laughed it off. Me? With a dog? I've never owned a dog. Dogs are for people who know how to stay in one place and who don't consider reheating frozen lasagna a culinary triumph. But the idea wouldn't go away. It stuck in my brain like that one Pharrell Williams song you can't escape at the grocery store - that sticks in your mind like chewing gum on hot asphalt. You need a dog *"Because [you'll be] happy... Clap along if you feel like happiness is the truth..."*

Suddenly, I was imagining a furry companion curled up next to me during those long, snowy winters, keeping me warm while I binge-read mystery novels, and muttered things like, "Who *really* killed the ancient aunti for her money, huh?" A dog wouldn't judge me for talking to myself or eating nachos for dinner. A dog would just... be there. Loyal. Steady. Enthusiastically wagging his tail because I exist and occasionally throw treats his way.

Of course, I immediately envisioned the *perfect* dog. None of those tiny, yappy purse-dogs for me. I wanted a big dog. A dog with a sturdy build and soulful eyes. A dog that could handle the winters here and still have enough energy to kayak with me in the summer—because yes, in this fantasy, my dog is also an outdoorsy adventurer who respects my need for someone to motivate me to get off the couch and out of the house.

But let's be real. Getting a dog is a *commitment*. A dog isn't just a cute sidekick; it's a full-time job with fur. You can't halfheartedly own a dog the way you halfheartedly water a houseplant and then hope it'll pull through. Yet, as I stood there staring out at Legacy Lake, watching an osprey swoop down and snatch a fish like I was watching a perpetual nature channel without the commercials, I couldn't shake the feeling that maybe a dog was exactly what I needed. A dog wouldn't care about my flaws or my lack of direction. It wouldn't ask if I was dating or why I didn't have a retirement plan. A dog would just... love me. And maybe bark at ghosts and raccoons.

So now, as I stand here contemplating my future— jobless, manless, middle-aged, possibly abnormally paranormal—I'm starting to think that a dog might be the most stable relationship I could manage right now. Sure, it's a bit of a cliché, but who cares? Life is short, the lake is beautiful, and I might as well share it with someone who will never judge me for eating a whole pint of Ben & Jerry's Cherry Garcia in my pajamas, in front of the tv. Even if that someone drools a lot and sheds all over the furniture. Honestly, I think I'd be okay with that.

I suppose I'm really searching for something beyond becoming a dog's pooper scooper. A purpose, maybe? Not just a companion? A reason to stick around long enough to learn which neighbors leave their Christmas lights up year-round? Whatever it is, it's out there somewhere, just out of reach.

This place, though—this life—it has a peculiar way of demanding some deep, existential transformation from all of us from time to time. But let's be honest: Transformation isn't a dramatic cinematic moment with a triumphant soundtrack. It's more like awkwardly stumbling into the next version of yourself.

Anyway, I plopped down on my secondhand couch—the kind that has seen better days but still hugs you like it means it—with my feet up on an ottoman that's about three wobbly screws away from disaster. My laptop flickered to life and I checked my email. Oh! an email from Maggie.

Ah, Maggie. My one local connection. She's the kind of friend who'd tell you to eat kale because it'll fix your soul, but who will also bring over a bottle of wine to wash the taste of it out of your mouth when you inevitably spit it out. Maggie lives on Liberty Ridge, overlooking the lake, in a house that screams "Pacific Northwest Zen." She's a holistic vet with an office so feng shui, it feels like a day spa for stressed-out Labradoodles. Enlightened pet owners adore her. Traditional vets want to chase her out of town with pitchforks. But Maggie doesn't care. Maggie has a husband, John, who's a real estate attorney—a fact that keeps the pitchforks firmly in the shed.

Her subject line was simple but oddly prescient: **"Looking for a furry friend?"**

Naturally, I opened it. And oh my, Maggie knows how to stage a destiny ambush.

Hi Kat,

I hope the cabin's everything you dreamed it would be — peaceful, quiet, beautiful views, and absolutely zero dire newscasts. I've been thinking about you out there on your own and just wanted to remind you that you're welcome to come over anytime. Seriously. No need to call or worry you're intruding. John and I are thrilled you're here!

BTW, something serendipitous came up. My neighbors, the Johnsons, just had a litter of Portuguese Water Dogs, and as soon as I saw them, I thought of you. Knowing how much you love kayaking and swimming, I figured, well... to put it bluntly: you need a dog. And you're both of Portuguese heritage – so you share a common kinship. Kindof...

There's one in particular I think you'd love. He's a little brown-and-white guy with a streak of white down his muzzle—like he tripped into a bucket of paint. The Johnsons are calling him "Sir Galahad".

He's got a great temperament—adventurous enough to explore, but loyal enough to come running the second you call him. I've attached a video. No pressure, of course, but I thought you'd like to see him. If you're interested, I'd be happy to bring him over. I know you've never had a dog, but I'm here to help. You've got me as your puppy mentor, and you know I'm a total expert on PWDs.

Mags

I SAT THERE STARING at the email, smiling like a fool who just got handed a lifetime supply of happiness. Then I clicked the video attachment. And oh, sweet dog biscuits, there he was.

The camera focused on a fluffy ball of puppy love, his fur perfectly symmetrical brown with white chest and paws, his nose streaked with the most endearing splash of white paint. And his eyes—his eyes were pure puppy perfection, all curiosity and earnestness, like he was saying, "Hello, I'm here to fix your life. Do you have treats?"

I watched as he bumbled around the grass, nose to the ground, investigating every blade like it held the secrets of the universe. Then he looked up, as if remembering, *Oh, right! The human's filming me!* He trotted back toward the camera with the kind of enthusiasm that could make even the most hardened cynic go, "Awww!" His gaze fixed on the person with an expression of utter trust and eagerness. His little tail wagged so hard I worried it might fly off like a helicopter blade.

I watched the video again, and then again, my heart melting into a puddle. This little guy—*Sir Galahad,* knight of the backyard realm—was perfect. I could already picture our future together: morning walks by the lake, paw prints in the snow, him curled up by the fire while I read some tragic literary novel and wept unashamedly into his fur.

Of course, I knew I was romanticizing. Puppies aren't all tail wags and Instagram moments. They're messy, unpredictable, and occasionally insane. What if Sir Galahad turned out to be a water-hating Portuguese *Land* Dog? Or worse, what if he had the energy of a toddler on espresso? Or a land shark gnawing on everything, chewing my hand to pieces. Puppies don't come with instruction manuals—or mute buttons – or an off switch.

But none of that mattered. The fantasy was too sweet to resist. My fingers hovered over the keyboard, then started typing before I could overthink it.

Maggie!

YESSS!!!! I think....Thank you for thinking of me—and for sending that video. Oddly enough, I was just thinking about getting a dog. Fate? Or just your sneaky way of pushing me into puppy ownership?

I watched the video, and wow—Sir Galahad is adorable! I already feel like he's exactly the companion I need. Let's set up a visit. If he's even half as wonderful in person as he is on video, I think we're going to be a perfect match.

Since you're basically the Yoda of PWDs and a vet, I'll need all your advice. When can I meet him? BTW – do you offer a friends and family discount on vet services? (Joking...not joking.) 😄

Kat

WITH A DEEP BREATH, I hit send and leaned back on the couch. The cabin was still quiet, but it didn't feel quite so empty anymore. Soon, there would be the sound of paws on the floor, a wagging tail thumping against the furniture, and a new little soul to share this place with.

For the first time in years, I felt like I wasn't just passing through. Legacy Lake didn't feel like a stopover. It felt like home. Well, it would. As soon as Sir Galahad moved in and infused me with a constant contact high of oxytocin.

2

YAPPY HOUR

Two days later, as the sun dipped below the horizon and bathed the cabin in that gorgeous orange glow that looks like the sky decided to pour itself a tequila sunrise, Maggie arrived. She stepped out of her cargo van looking like a pint-sized superhero—Sir Galahad tucked under one arm, a pizza box in the other, and an expression that said, *I may look cheerful, but I'm exhausted, and this pizza is the only thing keeping me upright.*

Maggie had that confident vibe and stride of someone who's always had a dog trotting beside her. She was wearing jeans and a cute brown T-shirt that somehow fit her perfectly, because of course it did. No jewelry, though. Makes sense. You can't wear dangly earrings when you spend your working life handling angry cats that fixate on swaying shiny things and want nothing more than rip them right out of your ear. Her short, dark hair was sprinkled with just enough gray to make her look like she'd won a few battles in the war of adulthood, but not like she was losing the war entirely.

Trailing behind her was Sunshine, her own more traditionally colored black and white, curly haired Portuguese Water Dog, moving with the kind of regal air that only comes from knowing you're the undisputed favorite child. Sunshine stopped just long enough to sniff a patch of dirt near my porch, then gave a satisfied *sniff of approval,* as if to say, *Yeah, this place needs a dog.*

"Kat!" Maggie called, hefting the squirming Sir Galahad, who blinked in surprise at the sound of her voice. "I've brought your dog. And half the Pawsitive Connections pet store, apparently." She tilted her head toward the back seat, where I could see what appeared to be a tote bag containing the canine version of a survival kit: blankets, bowls, food, and—was that a bell? Maggie smirked like someone who knew she'd gone overboard but didn't care because *this is what responsible puppy mentorship looks like, dang it.*

I watched her handle Sir with a mix of maternal affection and a confidence that said, *I've done this before, and you, rookie, have not.* And she was right. She also knew I was freshly kind-of-retired—freshly dropped into that strange, undefined limbo society calls "the golden years," where I was *supposed* to be climbing Machu Picchu or corrupting grandchildren with candy and no bedtime. Instead, here I was, standing on my porch, about to become a puppy mom for the first time, with a mixture of excitement and panic bubbling in my heart. And she knew she needed to ease my anxiety.

I grabbed the tote bag and Maggie carried Sir into the house where I took the pizza box from her outstretched hand and put it and the bag on the kitchen island counter. "I know you have wine," she said, shooting me a look that was half-celebratory, half-let's-just-get-through-this. "But I brought a bottle of bubbly. It's inside the tote bag. This is a moment to celebrate!"

Maggie set Sir down on the floor, where he immediately started sniffing everything with the determination of a tiny, furry crime scene investigator. Within a few seconds, Sir trotted over to inspect me. When I bent down to greet him, he stopped and looked at me—really *looked* at me—with those round, intelligent puppy eyes that seemed to say, *Hey, lady, I think we're going to be friends.* Then, as if sealing the deal, he licked my hand in what can only be described as the canine equivalent of a handshake.

And just like that, I was a goner. "Well, I guess you're moving in permanently. Welcome home, Sir," I murmured, rubbing his soft little head.

Maggie caught my moment of puppy-induced awe and smiled knowingly as she turned her attention to the tote. "In here," she announced in her best *holistic vet voice,* "are the essentials." She started pulling out items like a magician pulling rabbits out of a hat. "Powder-blue fleece blanket—it smells like his mom to help with the transition. Two bowls. A bag of puppy food. And some frozen meat stew toppers."

At the word "food," Sir decided it was a good time to squat. Maggie moved faster than a caffeinated ninja, scooping him up mid-stream and plopping him onto the linoleum. "Not on the carpet, buddy," she said, as if she were talking to an old friend who'd made a harmless mistake. Meanwhile, I grabbed a dishcloth to mop up the evidence, marveling at her timing. *If this were me alone,* I thought, *that puddle would've been the size of the lake before I even noticed.*

As I wiped up the mess, Maggie pulled a book and an envelope from the tote and waved them at me like they were sacred texts. "All your need-to-know info is in here," she said. "Feeding schedule, potty training tips, vaccine stuff—parvo shots are non-negotiable, by the way. Oh, and a potty bell."

"A what now?" I asked, looking up from my cleanup efforts.

Maggie grinned as she pulled out a wide ribbon with bells sewn onto it, looping it over the doorknob. "A potty bell. You shake it to teach him to associate the sound with going outside. Then, when he figures out that ringing it makes the door open, you praise him and give him a treat. Eventually, he'll hit the bell on his own when he needs to go."

She gave the bells a little jingle, and Sir perked up, his ears twitching like someone had just said the magic word. Maggie immediately rewarded him with a treat from her pocket, grinning like she'd just performed a magic trick. "See? It's all about positive reinforcement."

I nodded, trying to absorb the avalanche of information. "Okay. I can do this. But only if I have a drink in hand while I learn. I'll grab the flutes. You uncork the bubbly."

And that's how my first night as a puppy mom began—with champagne, a stack of training tips, and Sir Galahad exploring his new home, blissfully unaware of the chaos he was about to bring into my usually uneventful life. But as I watched him wag his little tail and chase a dust bunny under the couch, I couldn't help but feel that this was exactly what I needed. Chaos often breeds its own kind of joy.

WE SETTLED ONTO THE FLOOR, backs against the couch I'd panic-bought the day I moved in, a purchase made purely on the basis of "this one's cheap, and they'll deliver right now." Sunshine stretched out by Maggie's feet, her usual spot, watching over Sir Galahad who pranced around like a tiny explorer, sniffing everything with the enthusiasm of someone who just discovered a new world. After a few minutes, his bouncy energy started to wane, and he blinked sleepily, clearly wondering where on earth he was supposed to crash.

I grabbed his little blanket and laid it out beside me. One sniff, and he made his decision, trotting over, flopping onto his back, and promptly passing out. His back legs splayed open in an unbothered sprawl, his front paws stretched straight toward the heavens like he'd just keeled over mid-revival.

"Wow," I said, grinning as I looked at the absurdly dramatic pose. "Dead cow?"

"It's the *Portie pose*," Maggie replied matter-of-factly.

"Portie?"

"Short for Portuguese Water Dog. They love sleeping on their backs like this—legs akimbo, spine all twisted, belly exposed to the world, and front paws either curled in like they're begging or sticking straight out like they're waiting for the rapture. It's basically their signature move."

We burst out laughing because, honestly, how could you not? I lifted my glass in a toast. "To Portie poses and a yappy, dappy, happy hour!"

Maggie clinked her glass with mine, her eyes twinkling. "Cheers to that. So, do you think you'll change his name?"

"I think I have to change it," I said. "It just doesn't suit either of us."

"Why not? Imagine the fun of yelling, 'Sir! Sir!' at the dog park. Every man within a hundred yards would turn around, wondering if you were addressing *him*. Instant icebreaker! Who knows? You might even meet someone worth your time. Dogs are great at discerning character, you know."

"So, if Sir snarled at a man, I should steer clear and if he licks him, I should lick him too?"

"Check for a wedding ring first!" she shot back, laughing. "Speaking of wedding rings... thought much about dating again? Or thought about changing your name back to your maiden name? Turning back the clock of life from Kat Drexler back to Kat Morai?"

I sighed and took a sip of wine. "I should go back to my maiden name. I'll think about it. It's kind of - well – neither name suits me anymore. I'm no longer a Drexler but I'm far from feeling like I fit in that old childhood surname. But I probably will. It seems like a good idea – to get a fresh start – a do-over and make a better choice in finding my person. But finding another man is demoralizing.

"Let's just say I've dabbled in the cesspool of online dating and checked out profiles of the local yokels before I moved here. Around here, the typical guy's profile falls in one of three categories.

First Category – 'I'm a narcissist looking for a younger model to worship me.' Category 2 is 'I'm a golfer with a lifetime supply of Viagra and willing to share my bed by not my money.' And Category 3 goes something like this..." I straightened up, slapped on my best redneck drawl, and launched into my impression:

"I gotta ATV, slight beer gut, never traveled but want you to take me there, anywhere. Graduated high school, live on my boat or in my trailer. Work construction when I can get work. Perfect woman for me? Must be tall, thin, beautifuuulll in all the right places, love to cuddle, financially secure (with enough for me). Love to camp. Longest relationship? Three years—lied about two of those. Had a dog for three years. You think you'll last three years? I'm in

---

We were laughing so hard by the end of it that tears streamed down our faces. I had to run to the bathroom to avoid peeing my pants.

"But wait, it gets better!" I said, still breathless as I ran back into the room and plopped back down. "The photos, Maggie. Oh, the photos. Picture this: shirtless guy, man boobs on full display, greasy old baseball hat perched on his head, holding up a dead fish like it's the biggest thing he's been proud of in years. So sexy."

Maggie howled. "What's more attractive—the man boobs or the fish?"

"Definitely the man boobs. Nothing gets me hotter than a pair of pecs that double as flotation devices," I shot back. "But seriously, they're always grinning like they just won the lottery. Half the time, the fish are so tiny they might as well be bait. The other half, the fish are these massive, like something out of a sci-fi movie. Why pictures of fish? What's the message here?"

"Bigger is better?" Maggie suggested innocently.

"Apparently! But then there are the medium fish guys. They're my favorite. Not too big, not too small, just... a nice, respectable trout or bass. It's like they're saying, 'Hey, look, I caught this. Maybe I can catch you? Anyway, fish pixs beat photos of selfies taken in the bathroom mirror without their shirts on. It's kind of all American boyhood cute.'"

"Maybe you should avoid the fish guys altogether," Maggie said, still laughing. "Find someone with a dog instead. Animal lovers are better."

"Why not a cat guy?" I asked, raising an eyebrow.

Maggie leaned back, smirking. "Cat guys are a whole different ball game. They're not bad, but do you *really* want to date someone whose entire emotional support system fits in a litter box?"

"At least the cat's alive and not hanging from a fish hook." And with that, I poured us both another glass of wine and toasted to the ridiculousness of modern dating, dogs, and the fact that, no matter what, we'd always have laughter to lighten our days.

The conversation unraveled into other giggles and tangents, as conversations fueled by wine and puppy cuteness tend to do, until the empty bottle on the table reminded us it was time to call it a night. Maggie had to work tomorrow, and I had to prepare for my first sleepless night as a brand-new puppy mom. Apparently, this involved waking up every few hours to escort Sir outside for a pee, like some kind of nocturnal butler. Exactly what I'd envisioned for retirement.

Maggie retrieved a crate from the car and we set it up in a cozy corner of the room, filled one of his bowls with water. Then she gave me a crash course in puppy pads and crate training. She talked quickly and confidently, and I stood there nodding along, trying to keep up, while silently wondering if I should be taking notes—or hiring a live-in nanny.

"Patience is key," she said, glancing down at Sir, who had swapped his dramatic dead-cow sleeping pose for something resembling a tiny, tightly curled croissant. His powder-blue blanket was bunched up under his nose like a pillow, and his little paws were tucked under his chin like he'd just settled in for a long winter's nap.

"He's only nine weeks old. There'll be accidents, probably some whining, maybe even a tantrum or two. Stick to a routine, though, and he'll settle in soon enough. And remember, you can call or text me anytime. Literally anytime."

I tried to muster confidence. "How bad could it be? I mean, how much chaos can a puppy this small really create?"

Maggie grinned, her eyes sparkling with the mischief of someone who knows exactly what kind of chaos is coming. "Oh, you'll see. You might as well start calling him Sir Pees-a-Lot now and save yourself the trouble later."

I laughed, but there was a flicker of doubt in the back of my mind. I turned serious for a moment, glancing at Sir, his tiny body rising and falling with each peaceful breath. "You know," I admitted, "I always thought I'd spend my retirement traveling. I had this vague idea—get a home base, join a community, then spend my springs in Europe, my winters scuba diving somewhere warm. A dog wasn't... part of the plan."

Maggie tilted her head, her expression soft but steady. "Are you sure about the puppy, Kat? I mean, really sure? Because if you're not, it's better to know now—within the next couple of days before he gets really bonded to you."

I didn't answer right away. My eyes wandered back to Sir, fast asleep, completely vulnerable and trusting, as if he knew I'd take care of him no matter what. And in that moment, something stirred in me—something I hadn't felt in years. For so long, I'd told myself I wasn't the nurturing type. I didn't need family or children, didn't want the weight of responsibility tying me down. I was independent, ambitious, and career-driven. But now, watching this tiny creature curl into himself with such contentment, I wondered if I'd been lying to myself all along.

"I don't regret it," I said slowly, almost to myself. "But it does feel... strange. Like I've been in survival mode and holding my breath for so long, and now I realize I can exhale."

Maggie studied me for a long moment, her expression inscrutable, the way it always is when she's piecing together something she already knows about you before you've admitted it to yourself. "You know," she said finally, her voice quiet but sure, "some people think getting a dog is practice for having kids. But I think it's the other way around. Sometimes, choosing a dog is the first time we choose to let ourselves love and be loved without conditions or complications. No screaming toddlers. No rebellious teenagers. No demanding husband. Just love—simple, honest, and constant."

She glanced down at Sunshine, who was waiting patiently at her side, ready to leap into the van for the short ride home. I walked Maggie to the door, and we stepped outside into the night. The sky had deepened to a velvety blue, the stars just starting to prick through the darkness, and the lake shimmered faintly, reflecting the moonrise.

"We're not doing it wrong, you know," Maggie said, her voice soft but certain, as if reading my thoughts. "This whole thing—staying put, finding a sense of community instead of ticking off bucket-list trips—it's not a waste. It takes courage to stay in one place and build something lasting."

I nodded, letting her words settle over me. Maybe she was right. Maybe staying—here, in this rickety old cabin with its fading paint and moss-covered roof—was its own kind of adventure. One I hadn't planned but needed.

But then, just as Maggie was about to leave, a flicker of panic bubbled up in my chest. "There's one small problem," I blurted out, my voice softer than I'd intended. "I, uh, haven't actually asked my landlord if I can have a dog."

The confession hung in the air for a moment, heavy but

ridiculous. Maggie turned to me, raised an eyebrow, and then looked at the cabin, taking in the weathered wood siding, the crooked porch steps, and the general vibe of *charmingly neglected lake shack.*

"Kat," she said, biting back a laugh, "look around. Do you really think your landlord cares? This place should be grateful it has a tenant at all. And let's face it, this is temporary. You're not staying here forever. You'll figure out what you want—whether it's a better house or a permanent spot at Legacy Lake. For now, enjoy the view. And the dog. I mean, how could anyone say no to that face?"

She had a point. Maybe Maggie was right—this old cabin, this new life, this tiny, trusting puppy... maybe it wasn't the plan. But maybe it was exactly what I needed for now.

I tried to smile, but the unease lingered, sticking to me like lake humidity on a summer evening. Maggie was probably right—this cabin was as rustic as it gets, more charming for its setting than for any actual maintenance. I mean, if you squinted just right, the peeling paint and sagging porch steps could almost look...quaint.

I'd rented it sight unseen, which, in hindsight, might not have been my smartest move. The entire process had been weirdly impersonal—just a few phone calls, an online lease, and then boom, I showed up with my boxes and dreams of lakeside tranquility. The landlord, Oliver, had been polite enough on the phone, but there was something about his tone that stuck with me. He had this *aw, shucks* good-old-boy vibe at first, the kind of folksy charm that makes you picture him wearing overalls and fixing fences.

But once we agreed on the rental price, his voice shifted. Beneath the friendliness was a sharp, precise edge, like a razor blade hidden in a pillow. It was as if he wasn't just renting me a cabin but entrusting me with some sacred artifact. He made it abundantly clear: no disturbances, no changes to the cabin, no tampering with the property. And then he'd dropped the kicker: *This is my home. Not yours.*

Whoa.

At the time, I'd shrugged it off. I was too eager to start my lakeside retirement adventure to worry about the landlord's quirks. But now, with Sir curled up inside, blissfully unaware of the world's complications, I couldn't shake the nagging thought that Oliver might not be thrilled about my new furry roommate.

Maggie must have sensed my tension because she rested a hand on my shoulder, grounding me in the way only a good friend can. "Kat, you're overthinking this," she said softly, her voice steady and reassuring. "You've been wanting a companion for years. You finally have one. A good one, at that—he's not going to leave his socks all over the floor or steal the covers." She paused, her smile faint but confident. "Do you really think Oliver's going to care? He probably lives miles away and hasn't thought about this cabin in years. If he even notices—which he probably won't—you'll deal with it then. Trust me, this place is way off his radar."

I nodded, trying to let her words sink in. Maggie had a way of making everything sound manageable, like life's problems could be solved with a little common sense and a glass of wine. But still, a small part of me couldn't shake the unease. Being a renter always came with that unsettling limbo—like you're living in a house you can't quite call home. Everything feels temporary, always under someone else's control.

I sighed, staring out at the lake, the moonlight dancing on its surface. Maybe Maggie was right. Maybe Oliver wouldn't notice, wouldn't care, wouldn't storm in demanding an eviction. But even as I told myself that, the words *This is my home, not yours* echoed faintly in my mind, like the creak of old wood settling into the night.

3

TROUBLE UNLEASHED

The morning sun filtered through the cabin windows, scattering golden patches of light across the floor, the kind of lighting you see in coffee commercials that makes you believe mornings can actually be pleasant. "First things first, puppy," I said, giving the bells by the door a shake before opening it. "Go potty!" To my utter amazement, he trotted out like a seasoned professional and did his business.

I stood there marveling at how much liquid one tiny puppy could produce, debating whether to treat him or just move on to breakfast. Breakfast won.

Energized by his meal, Sir transformed into a tiny whirl-wind, exploring the cabin as if he'd been born to it. He trotted from room to room, tail wagging and paws tapping against the old wood floors, claiming every nook and cranny —and my heart—with an effortless confidence that seemed far too big for his tiny body.

Just as I started fixing a cup of coffee, finally feeling like I might actually settle into this whole domesticity thing, a loud series of knocks shattered the peace. Sir's head snapped up, ears at full alert, and before I could stop him, he bolted to the door, his paws skittering across the floor like a cartoon character mid-chase.

I opened the door to find a man standing on the porch. He was short and slightly hunched, with a shock of white hair sticking out at odd angles like he'd just walked through a wind tunnel—or perhaps lost a fight with a pair of scissors. His plaid shirt hung loose on his frame, and his jeans were frayed at the hem. He looked like he'd wandered out of a fairytale where trolls disguise themselves as withered lumberjacks.

"Katherine, right?" he said, smiling vaguely, his expression hovering somewhere between pleasant and perpetually confused. "I'm Oliver. I own the cabin."

Oh, great. *Oliver.* The landlord who thought giving 24 hours' notice was optional and lived far, far away. I forced a smile, masking my annoyance. Who just *shows up* unannounced at 8 a.m.? Didn't we have rules for this sort of thing?

Sir, oblivious to my internal monologue, seized the moment to bolt outside, tail wagging furiously. He skidded to a stop at Oliver's feet, plopped his tiny butt down, and stared up at him with wide, innocent eyes that screamed, *Hi! I live here now. Pet me.*

"Oh, I see you've got yourself a little...um... friend," Oliver said, peering down at Koa like he was inspecting a science experiment. "What's his name?"

"Uh... Sir for now," I said, glancing down at my tiny traitor, who continued gazing at Oliver with the unabashed enthusiasm of a used-car salesman closing a deal.

Oliver stared at him, unmoved. Not even a pat on the head. Just a slow, ponderous nod, like someone contemplating whether this dog-shaped problem was worth addressing. "Well," he said, straightening up with a labored sigh, "I just thought I'd drop by to say hello. Welcome you to Legacy Lake. We're a friendly bunch here, you know."

Based on the way he studied Sir, I wasn't so sure about that.

He shifted on his feet, gesturing vaguely in the direction of the lake. "We even have a monthly wine-tasting party, right at my place. You should come by this Friday. It's the best way to meet the neighbors."

"Oh, that's kind of you," I replied, resisting the urge to shut the door and hide under the bed. The last thing I wanted was to be tossed into a crowd of strangers, but Oliver's face was so earnest it was impossible to say no. "I suppose I could stop by."

"Great, great!" he said, his enthusiasm making me regret every word. "Seven o'clock sharp. You will meet some neighbors there. Brenda and Sam will be there—lovely folks. And Evie. She's a character, you'll see. You'll fit right in."

Before I could muster a polite excuse, Sir decided it was time to assert his dominance. He trotted over to Oliver's right foot, squatted, and let loose a steady stream of pee.

"SIR!" I yelped, nudging him away just as he started gearing up for an even bigger act of defiance.

Oliver glanced down at his now-damp shoe, his face darkening as if he'd just discovered the true meaning of betrayal. "Well," he said, his tone clipped. "See you Friday night. I'll text you the address."

With that, he shuffled back toward his car, one leg shaking off the piddle every few steps, muttering something under his breath that I couldn't quite catch.

"I'm so sorry!" I called after him, trying to sound cheerful. "Looking forward to it!"

He didn't turn around, just gave a little wave over his

shoulder, as though dismissing me—and Sir—from his thoughts entirely.

Once he disappeared down the driveway, I scooped Sir up and pressed him close, shaking my head. "Well, buddy, I think we dodged that one. Barely."

Still, a faint unease lingered. There was something about Oliver's unannounced visit that didn't sit right with me. And why didn't he like dogs?

I thought about Bill Murray's wisdom on the matter: *"I'm suspicious of people who don't like dogs, but I trust a dog when it doesn't like a person."*

As the puppy nuzzled into my chest, I decided that if Oliver ever came back unannounced, Sir would be ready. With more than just a bladder full of ammunition as he made very clear his feelings towards Oliver.

LATER THAT DAY, I decided to take Sir for a proper walk. Unleashed. Because really, how fast and far could a puppy go? Famous last words.

He trotted ahead of me along the spur road connecting five houses built close together, overlooking the lake in addition to mine, his tiny tail held high like a victory flag. Every bush, tree, and random patch of grass demanded his attention, each one sniffed with the intensity of a detective on a hot lead. His fearless confidence struck a chord in me, a faint echo of the self-assurance I used to feel in my working years. Now that I wasn't working, I felt unmoored, unsure of who I was without the labels of career or spouse to ground me. It wasn't a feeling I enjoyed.

At the end of the road, a small house built into the hillside came into view, its tiny brick front yard leading down a few stairs to their main door. Before I could call him back,

Sir bolted down the entry steps like an Olympic sprinter, making a beeline for the open door. I dashed after him, hoping to stop him before he invaded someone's kitchen or —heaven forbid—peed on their rug.

A woman appeared in the doorway, mid-sixties, with long, thick and curly, salt-and-pepper hair and the kind of calm, no-nonsense energy that instantly commands respect. She was my height, about 5'3", with a rosy glow to her cheeks and laugh lines around her eyes that suggested a life well-lived. Behind her, I spotted an older man with a shock of white hair rising from a recliner. He moved toward the door, smiling faintly.

"Looks like we've got a visitor," the woman said, her voice warm with amusement.

Before I could stammer out an apology, Sir reappeared, triumphantly holding a stuffed toy in his mouth like a trophy.

"Well, I see you found the toy basket," the woman said, crouching down to give the pup a thorough scratch behind the ears. He leaned into her touch, his tail wagging so hard I worried it might detach.

"I'm so sorry," I managed, my words tumbling over themselves as he happily bit down on the squeaker hidden in the toy.

She waved a hand dismissively. "Don't worry about it. We're dog people."

Her husband, dressed in surfer board shorts and a navy T-shirt, ambled into view, his grin widening as he leaned against a counter. "Oh yeah, we've had dogs for years. In fact, Squirt—our black lab—should be around here somewhere."

"I'm Kat Drexler. Just moved into the little red cabin," I said, finally catching my breath. "And this is Sir for now."

"Surfernow? Unusual name. Welcome to the neighborhood," the woman said, straightening up. "I'm Brenda Harding, and this is my husband Sam."

Before I could correct her on the puppy name, Sam gestured an invite for me to come in and then edged toward a large Mac screen open to a photo editing program. "Hmm... Forgot to close this out."

"Are you a photographer?" I asked, curious.

"Former commercial photographer," he said. "Now I focus on wildlife photography. I was working on some underwater shots from a recent dive trip."

Brenda chimed in, "I used to own a bakery in town—pretty famous before I sold it. Now I have time for quilting and gardening."

I liked them instantly. She reminded me of Lily Tomlin, same voice inflection and mannerisms, similar look and I'd bet a similar irreverent sense of humor. Brenda's easy warmth and Koa's instant acceptance of her won me over. And Sam's quiet, observant demeanor reminded me of someone who's spent a lifetime behind the lens, letting the world see what he saw unfolding in front of him. He looked the part, too—his wiry frame and deeply tanned skin bore the marks of decades spent outdoors, his face lined from squinting into sunlight and camera viewfinders. They fit together and obviously loved each other deeply.

Brenda moved gracefully around the kitchen, pulling a treat from a cupboard with the practiced ease of someone who used to juggle hot trays and impatient customers. She knelt down and commanded, "Sit," holding the treat over Koa's head until his little butt hit the floor.

"Good sit," she said, handing him the treat and glancing up at me with a smile. "What kind of dog is he? Doodle of some sort?"

"Not a doodle. A Portuguese Water dog."

"Oh like the Obama's had! Although I doubt they had much to do with raising him or feeding him for that matter."

I laughed.

"So," she said, "I saw Oliver out walking your way earlier. I take it you met Oliver and got an invite to his wine party?"

Sam leaned forward slightly, his eyes fixing on mine, as if trying to gauge my reaction.

"Yes," I replied cautiously. "He stopped by this morning. Very... welcoming. In a sort of invasive way."

Brenda raised an eyebrow, her expression shifting ever so slightly. "Oh, he's welcoming, alright," she said, her tone casual but with a hint of something sharper. "Just... keep your guard up around him, that's all."

I hesitated, unsure what she meant, but Sam chuckled and added, "Yeah, Oliver's always got his nose in everyone's business, but don't expect him to fix anything. He's more about offering help than actually following through."

Good intel to have. Sir, sensing the shift in mood, wagged his tail and nuzzled Brenda's hand for another treat. I told them about Sir's earlier mishap with Oliver's shoe, and they laughed, Sam declaring, "Little Sir's trouble unleashed—and clearly an excellent judge of character."

As I turned to leave, Brenda said, "You know, we have driveway parties from time to time. They start as we get to talking and then we just pull up chairs and tune into cocktail hour. If you see us out, join us."

"I will," I said, smiling. "And I hope to meet Squirt next time!"

Brenda exchanged a glance with Sam, something subtle and unspoken passing between them. "Oh, Squirt must be napping upstairs," Sam said quickly, his tone light but unconvincing.

As Sir and I made our way back down the road, I

couldn't help but feel there was more to the story about Squirt—something they weren't saying like maybe their dog was ill. But I didn't push.

The houses on the hillside were close together, their driveways practically spilling into the narrow road. It was easy to see how these impromptu driveway gatherings could happen and I looked forward to joining in and getting the lowdown on the neighborhood.

But Brenda's parting words lingered. There was something about Oliver's insistence on the wine party, his casual charm, that reinforced my sense that felt something was slightly off, like a sour note in an otherwise pleasant melody.

Back at the cabin, Sir bounded ahead, his joy undimmed. I ruffled his fur, letting his energy wash away the unease, and together we stepped into the quiet sanctuary of home. Whatever secrets the lake and its people held, they could wait. For now, it was just me and pup, and that was enough.

4

DEATH UNCORKED

The invitation was unassuming—a simple, handwritten note tucked into my mailbox by Oliver himself:

Wine Tasting. Tonight, 7 PM. A friendly gathering of neighbors—hope to see you there!

No frills. No fancy font. Just an address scrawled underneath. I'd expected my landlord to be the kind of person who remained shrouded in mystery, living far away and only swooping in to deal with repairs or collect rent checks. Instead, he lived just two blocks down the road. Walking distance. Too close. *Yuck.*

As I got ready for the party, my nerves started to rise. It wasn't the prospect of meeting new neighbors that had me uneasy—it was the idea of being in *Oliver's* space. The cabin I rented already felt weirdly tied to him, like he was less of a landlord and more of a looming, ever-present warden. The whole setup gave me the creeps.

My only comfort was Koa, who was blissfully unaware of my social anxiety, curled up in his crate and snoring softly. I'd decided to leave him at home, hoping he wouldn't destroy the place or attempt a puppy jailbreak in my absence.

With a bottle of Prosecco in hand—because nothing says *I'm approachable but don't push your luck* like bubbly —I set off toward Oliver's house. The night was crisp, the stars just beginning to dot the sky, and the dirt road leading to his home was illuminated by the faint glow of the full moon. I took a deep breath, trying to convince myself this would all be fine.

When Oliver's house came into view, I almost tripped over my own feet. The place was sprawling, like someone had started with a cozy cottage and then haphazardly tacked on rooms as the mood struck. Architectural harmony? Not here. About ten yards from the driveway, I noticed a green gardening glove lying in the dirt, looking oddly abandoned. Playing the good neighbor, I picked it up and placed it on a bench near the porch before knocking on the door.

"Kat!" Oliver's voice boomed as he threw the door open. He spread his arms wide like he was about to hug me, but quickly thought better of it, stepped back and lowered them again. "So glad you could make it! Come in, come in!"

I plastered on my best *polite-but-not-too-friendly* smile and stepped inside. The house was... eclectic. A mix of cozy and chaotic, with mismatched furniture and trinkets that screamed *antiques my mother left me!* None of them of any value – I noted with my practiced way of sizing up antiques – an occupational habit that I probably won't ever break. But the flower arrangements displayed in various antique-looking vases were stunning. The sweet and sultry scent of lilies dominated one area of the room while the fresh and soft scent of heirloom roses wafted around the room each time the door opened and a new guest arrived.

GUESTS WERE SCATTERED throughout the living room, sipping wine and chatting in clusters. I spotted Brenda wearing a cute red shirt and tan capris and Sam in his characteristic board shorts and a mismatched 1960s Hawaiian aloha shirt near the unlit fireplace, lifting their glasses in a silent toast.

"Kat! Over here!" Brenda called, waving me over. "Come meet Claire and Ted! I've been telling them about you and Sir. They have the Great Dane, Pepper—just the kind of older bitch a young male needs to teach him how to be a dog."

I laughed. "I kinda thought boys grew up teaching each other how to be dogs. Horndogs at least. A little different in the canine kingdom having a bitch teach them boundaries right out of the gate!"

"You're going to fit right in," Brenda replied with a grin.

Claire, a tall middle-aged woman casually dressed in jeans and a stylish green tank top with a cream cardigan that seemed straight of an east coast catalog, stepped forward with a warm smile. She held a near empty glass of soda in one hand that she placed on a side table and a small plate of canapés in the other. "Good to meet you. This is my husband, Ted," she said, gesturing to a dark-haired man with a runner's physique whose green golf shirt all but shouted his favorite hobby.

Ted leaned in for a handshake, his easy demeanor and his height matching Claire's. "Welcome to the neighborhood. And don't worry about Koa wandering—if he makes it to our place, he'll be met by Pepper. She needs a puppy around to keep her young."

"I'm sure I'll be right behind him," I said. "He's my first dog, so I'm learning as I go."

Claire tilted her head in surprise. "First dog? Really?"

"Really," I admitted. "Now that I'm working from home, I finally have the time to dedicate to raising one. But any puppy-rearing advice is welcome."

Ted smiled, gesturing toward Claire. "She's your go-to. She knows dogs and is on the board of the local animal shelter."

"I'm more of an accountant than a dog trainer but I'd be happy to help," Claire added.

"Oh, thanks. I'm going to set this down and pour a drink," I said, holding up my bottle of Prosecco.

Claire leaned closer, lowering her voice. "Wait a minute. That's Marissa over there," she said, nodding toward a well-dressed woman making her way to the bar.

"Here come the fireworks," Brenda murmured, appearing at my side, sandwiching me between them. "She's a real estate developer—been trying to buy up this whole spur road to turn it into some exclusive community. Your cabin's high on her list."

I frowned. "Oliver won't sell, though, right?"

Brenda chuckled. "Not a chance. People have tried. They leave with their tails between their legs."

Sam joined us, standing behind Brenda and glancing toward Marissa. "She's already three sheets to the wind. Won't be long before she starts stirring the pot."

"Pity," he added. "She's beautiful, but she's her own worst enemy. Everything she does—drinking, dealing, scheming—she does in excess. It's only a matter of time before it catches up with her."

As I watched Marissa pour herself another glass of wine, her sharp movements betraying a practiced cool, I couldn't help but feel the room shift slightly. The energy around her seemed volatile, like a storm cloud hovering just above the horizon.

Ted returned, handing Claire a small bottle of Perrier, after noticing she had abandoned her can of soda. He nodded toward Marissa. "Wonder what she'll try tonight."

"Whatever it is, it won't work on Oliver," Brenda said. "He's stubborn as they come."

I laughed, though the tension in the room was palpable. Koa may not have been there to defuse the situation with his puppy antics, but I mentally noted to keep a closer eye on Oliver and Marissa. There was more to this wine party than meets the eye, and I had a feeling it wouldn't end quietly.

With a quiet sigh, I stood between my new neighbors, holding the bottle of Prosecco by the neck as if I were ready to chug from the bottle, curious to watch the neighborhood drama unfold like the opening act of a play I hadn't meant to attend.

Marissa stood by the counter, her posture rigid and her expression barely masking annoyance. She was dressed impeccably, of course—an unwrinkled tan linen blazer, a sleek black tank top, tailored tan slacks that ended just above a perfectly sculpted ankle, and just-sexy-enough two-inch heeled sandals. She looked like she'd stepped out of an ad for "corporate power with a dash of wine country chic."

Across from her, Oliver slouched in his mismatched khakis and plaid button down, hair barely combed, the human embodiment of "I don't care what you think." His relaxed posture was a façade, though. I'd already seen through his "aww shucks" exterior to the shrewd man underneath.

Their body language told the whole story. Marissa's clipped, restrained gestures suggested she was one wrong word away from snapping, while Oliver just smiled calmly, letting her irritation bounce right off him. I couldn't hear their words, but the tension between them hung in the air like a thunderstorm waiting to break.

A woman walked out of the kitchen and stood beside Oliver. She was petite, mid-50s, with artfully styled short, brown hair, Balayage with perfect high and low lights. She exuded a quiet confidence, the kind of person you just *know* has their act together. I leaned toward Brenda.

"Is that Oliver's wife? And more importantly, who does her hair? I need a referral."

Brenda chuckled. "That's Sandra, Oliver's sister. And you're not the first to ask about her hair. She's got an amazing garden, too. Look at the flower arrangements."

I glanced around the room. This time noting one stunning vase that looked like Baccarat Crystal filled with roses and rose buds. Another vase looked like a Dale Chihuly original in cobalt blue with yellow rim holding daisies, and ferns, arranged so beautifully they could have been in an architectural magazine spread. But the one I thought most beautiful was an antique silver pitcher holding a unique arrangement of Lily of the Valley interspersed with tall stalks of lavender and tall silvery dry stalks with little dried, red berries clinging along the sides.

"She also owns a lavender farm," Brenda continued. "Has a distillery in the basement where she makes lavender hydrosols. And dehydrates flowers as well. Strange setup, though—she and Oliver share the house. For some reason, Oliver rents out his own places but refuses to live in them."

Before I could respond, Oliver's voice rose above the din, catching everyone's attention.

"Over my dead body!" he practically shouted.

I turned just in time to see him glaring at Marissa, his calm demeanor gone.

"Or better yet—yours!" he added.

The room went quiet.

Marissa's face hardened, but she didn't back down. "Nothing you can do about it, Oliver. I've got the permits to develop the hillside overlooking your lake houses. You might as well sell me your properties below. I'll have lakefront property and beach access one way or another."

"This land has been in my family for generations," Oliver snapped. "I'll never sell. And neither will the neighbors! And there is a reason why we don't just let anyone have beach access. We pay high enough waterfront taxes to keep it all private. Someone wants a beach they can go jump in the river!"

Sandra placed a steadying hand on Oliver's arm and whispered something in his ear. With a sharp exhale, he turned and stormed into the kitchen, leaving the room buzzing with unspoken questions.

"True that. We'll never sell. By the way, that's Evie," Brenda said, pointing toward a tall woman who was now striding confidently toward Marissa. Her messy bun and multicolored silk shawl gave her a bohemian, almost mystical air, like a cross between a yoga instructor and a fortune teller.

"She's a naturopath," Brenda explained. "You'll probably see her foraging for mushrooms and plants when you're out walking Koa. When Koa gets a little older there are amazing trails close by and great for long walks. I'll tell you where they are later. Fireworks aren't over yet. Watch this."

Debating whether I should uncork the bottle and start chugging, I decided to wait. Evie stopped in front of Marissa, her voice firm but calm. "Marissa, take a chill pill and move on from this fantasy of owning the lake."

Reaching into her crossbody bag, Evie abruptly pulled out a small glass bottle and sprayed a mist around Marissa's head. The scent of lavender filled the air as everyone nearby stared in stunned silence.

Marissa's expression shifted from shock to indignation. "What the hell are you doing?"

"Relax," Evie said with a laugh. "It's lavender hydrosol. Sandra makes it. Calming, isn't it?" she added as she continued walking into the kitchen.

I leaned toward Brenda. "Borderline assault with a scented weapon. Bold move."

"It works, though," Brenda replied with a smirk.

Marissa muttered something under her breath and turned back to the counter, reaching for the nearest wine bottle.

I decided it was a good time to move to the opposite end of the counter from Marissa, where many bottles of wine, liqueurs and spirits had been set out like an open bar for people to mix their own drinks. A bucket of beer and ice and white wine bottles anchored the far end of the counter which meant I would have to be closer to Marissa than I wanted when I uncorked my bottle. I popped the cork on my Prosecco and poured myself a glass, savoring the first sip. But before I could enjoy the moment, Marissa sidled up next to me, her expression softening into something resembling politeness.

"Champagne?" she asked, eyeing my glass.

"Prosecco," I corrected.

"Good choice. Never could tolerate the local wines these people bring," she said, completely ignoring me as she grabbed my bottle and poured herself a full flute. The bubbles overflowed onto the counter, but she didn't seem to notice—or care. She gave me a faint, bemused shrug as if to say, *Oops, not sorry.* Then took a long, unsophisticated gulp, leaving a bright red lipstick stain on the rim.

Before I could respond, Sandra walked over holding out

a small plate of 3 mushroom canapés. She lay it on the counter in front of Marissa with a sweet but pointed smile.

"I believe you tried one this morning and liked it so here you go. My mother used to make these and paired it with a little sweet liquor. But I don't have...wait a minute," she turned away to open a side cupboard near the fridge and drew out a vintage looking Royale Deluxe Chambord Liqueur Crystal Bottle with a metal crown. "Ah! A Chambord Kir Royal! Perfect!" Then she turned to see Marissa holding out her glass of Prosecco, expectantly.

"Umm, yes please," Marissa mumbled as she munched on another canape.

As Sandra poured the sweet red raspberry liquor into her Prosecco flute, I stepped away quickly, taking my glass with me intending to mingle with the crowd. But a crash behind me of crystal shattering on the floor, and a distraught cry from Sandra caught my attention. Apparently, she had knocked over the bottle of Chambord after pouring Marissa's drink and she scurried back into a side room to fetch a broom and cleaning supplies.

The evening wore on in a strange, disjointed rhythm. Conversations ebbed and flowed, neighbors exchanged pleasantries, and Marissa alternated between sipping her drink and glaring at Oliver from across the room. I was just starting to relax and meeting others in the room when it happened.

Marissa's face suddenly twisted in confusion. The color drained from her cheeks as she clutched at her heart. Her glass slipped from her hand and shattered on the floor as her body convulsed.

"Marissa!" someone shouted.

She stumbled backward dramatic as an actress attempting to take center stage. Gasping for air, her arms flailed wildly, slapping at the air as if trying to fight off an invisible swarm of bees. Rising on her toes as if levitating, an open hand clutching her neck while her other hand closed into a fist and struck her own heart landing there with a small thud. After a split second, her tall, lean body gave a dramatic, full-body shudder that would've made the Alvin Ailey Dance Company proud — the kind where you're not sure if it's a medical emergency or just really bad interpretive dance of a heart attack in progress.

Then, as if the universe released her, she collapsed in a heap, limbs splaying out like a broken starfish – a dancer's finale memorializing the moment of death. For a moment, there was silence, the kind that makes you wonder if you should call for help or just back away slowly and pretend you didn't see anything.

But then, oh no, the pièce de résistance: froth bubbled up and pooled at the corners of her mouth, bubbling up like - well...reddish champagne bubbles. It was an oddly hypnotic sight, equal parts alarming and weirdly impressive, as if her mouth had decided to audition for a low-budget zombie film.

SHE LAY THERE, a masterpiece of chaos, while conversations from the far side of the room continued rising with laughter — blissfully unaware of the drama unfolding on the floor.

It took a few seconds before the shock abated and the room erupted into chaos.

"Call 911!" someone yelled.

Sam turned to Brenda and nodded towards a tall dark-haired man I'd see whizzing across the lake on a hydrofoil surfboard and said, "Richard is a doctor. I'll go get him."

"Not that kind of doctor," Brenda reminded him. "He's

an orthopedic surgeon and I doubt his wife would like it if he put his lips on Marissa's and gave her mouth to mouth."

"Good point." He surveyed the room again. "What about Frederick?"

She shook her head no. "Chiropractor – cracks backs. Not chests."

"What about Jan?" He noticed Jan shoving through the crowd, then abruptly hesitate when she looked down at Marissa.

"She's an oncologist. Wouldn't touch a foaming mouth with a 10-foot pole."

They looked over at Marissa whose writhing ceased just in time to see the volcano of burning red lava foam erupting from her mouth in earnest.

Just then, a younger woman pushed through the crowd, her movements sharp and purposeful. "Out of the way—I'm an ER nurse!"

"Thank God," Sam exclaimed.

I stood frozen; my glass clutched in a white-knuckled grip as the scene unfolded.

The nurse knelt beside Marissa; her face grim. "Toxic," she muttered. "No barrier for mouth-to-mouth. Chest compressions are all I can do until paramedics arrive."

As she began CPR, a sickening thought crept into my mind. This wasn't a heart attack or a seizure.

This was something much darker.

5

BOOZE AND BONES

My gaze shifted to the Prosecco bottle Marissa had poured from, and a wave of dread hit me like a linebacker on caffeine. Had someone tampered with it? My stomach churned. I'd had a glass—an entire glass. What if I was next? Was this it? Death by bubbly? I set my glass on the counter, leaned against it, and braced myself for my inevitable collapse, wondering how long it would take for the poison to finish me off.

Would I foam at the mouth too? Should I lie down somewhere so I wouldn't look ridiculous flopping onto the floor like a dying fish? Maybe I should have brought a less conspicuous drink. Death by imported Prosecco seems so romantic at first—until the fizz turns fatal - and your body twerks against the carpet involuntarily for all to see.

Sandra, hearing the commotion, emerged from the kitchen with another plate of appetizers –and surveyed the scene before her. "Oh my God," she cried. And in her horror over seeing Marissa splayed out on the floor, accidentally knocked over several bottles of booze as she tossed the plate on the counter.

Before I could fully spiral into a full-on anxiety attack, a loud crash came through the front door.

"Squirt!" I thought I heard Sam yell, though I didn't see the black lab he claimed to own. What I *did* see was my little crate-Houdini scampering into the room, his tail wagging like a metronome set to "hyperactive". Pepper hurtled over him as if trying to avoid tripping over the puppy beneath his feet and in so doing, crashed right into a side table knocking over probably the most expensive vase of flowers in the house. Sir pranced through the chaos as if he were the guest of honor, oblivious to the paramedics, the shouting, and Marissa's very un-partylike collapse.

Pepper carried something long. Something pale. Something... oh no.

He dropped it at my feet, his huge chest puffed up with pride when Sir scurried over for a sniff and a lick and a bit of a chew.

It was a bone.

Not just any bone. As someone who's handled my fair share of oddities—human skeletons, taxidermy, mummified remains, you name it—I knew immediately that this wasn't some innocent dog-chew toy. It was long, thin, and suspiciously *human*-looking.

The room froze. Guests who had been sneaking out the door to avoid the drama turned back, curious. The doctor still pumping Marissa's chest paused, mid-compression, her brow furrowed as she eyed the bone. All eyes shifted to the small, white object lying starkly on the dark carpet, radiating bad juju like it was auditioning for the lead role in a true-crime documentary.

With the elegance of a bulldozer in a China shop, Pepper zeroed in on the bone, snatching it away from Sir.

And then it happened: a doggie tug-of-war.

Pepper growled and yanked. Sir growled back, latched onto the bone with all the ferocity his tiny body could muster, and refused to let go. The bone twisted and jerked as the two wrestled, growling until Pepper lifted his giant head and flung the little puppy flailing in mid-air across the room where he crashed into the back of the couch.

"Stop them!" someone shouted, but no one seemed eager to jump into the fray. Chairs tipped over. Wine glasses shattered. A woman's cane went flying, though thankfully her companion caught her before she toppled over.

Sir, vastly outmatched but clearly fueled by delusions of grandeur, ran back and latched on again with his teeth, refusing to surrender. Pepper swung her massive head, and again Sir flew high this time, twisting mid-flight with a yelp and landing—miraculously—in Oliver's outstretched arms.

Oliver, caught off guard, promptly dropped him. Sir hit the floor running, unleashed and now feral with fear, leaving a faint trail of puppy pee as he zigzagged through the chaos, no idea what to do or where to hide. Utterly panicked.

"Sam! Squirt!" I yelled, pointing at the black lab who'd appeared out of nowhere, barking like he was auditioning for *The Hound of the Baskervilles*. Sam stared at me, looking as confused as I felt, until I shouted, "Grab Squirt!"

Sam snapped into action, commanding Squirt to go home. The lab turned tail and bolted back into the night, his mission to add to the mayhem apparently complete.

Meanwhile, Pepper reclaimed the bone and thrashed it back and forth, knocking over another side table and scattering canapés across the room. Sir refocused, lunged for the bone again. Just as the paramedics arrived, their sirens silenced but their grim efficiency unmistakable, Ted sprang forward, grabbed Pepper's collar, and wrestled the bone away. Brenda darted in like a big bad momma slapping a gun out of hoodlum's hand, and scooped up Sir, holding him back as he squirmed and squeaky barked, his eyes still locked on the prize.

The bone lay on the floor, dirt and dog drool smeared across its surface. Its long, pale shape looked disturbingly out of place amid the spilled wine and shattered glasses.

"What... what is that?" someone whispered.

A heavy silence settled over the room as everyone stared at the bone. It wasn't just a bone. It was *a bone.* The kind you find in anatomy textbooks. Or, you know, in the opening grossness of that crime scene show Bones.

Sam, ever the voice of calm, stepped forward and cleared his throat. "Alright, folks, let's not jump to conclusions. It's just a deer bone. Coyotes are always dragging stuff like this around. Nothing unusual."

He bent down, scooped up the bone, and slipped it into the inside pocket of his jacket with the smoothness of someone who's very used to hiding inconvenient truths.

The guests murmured in agreement, nodding as if trying to convince themselves that Sam was right. But the uneasy glances they exchanged told me no one was buying it. Many left quickly, seeking to avoid the chaos and trauma of watching a local tended to by paramedics.

The paramedics crouched over Marissa, working furiously, but after a few minutes, the lead paramedic shook his head. "She's gone," he said softly.

The room exhaled as one. I looked around, catching Brenda's eye. She gave me a tight, grim look.

Sir, apparently sensing that the drama was over, wriggled free from Brenda's grip and trotted back to me, his tail wagging as if to say, *Wasn't that fun?*

I scooped him up, holding him close, as Oliver stepped

forward, his face pale and his jovial mask cracking under the weight of the night's events.

"Well," he said, his voice strained. "Looks like we've had quite an eventful night."

Understatement of the year.

6

KNOW THY NEIGHBORS

Let me tell you there's nothing quite like the sight of a perfectly tailored tan blazer wheeled out on a stretcher as paramedics suddenly realize they forgot to cover her with a sheet, to make you rethink your life choices. Just hours earlier, Marissa had been the queen of thinly veiled passive-aggression, cutting Oliver down with a glance and wielding her tailored power outfit like a sword. Now? She was, well... *gone.* And I was left wondering how this wine-tasting soirée had turned into a scene from an Agatha Christie novel.

The officer in charge, a tall man with the kind of clipped, no-nonsense demeanor that suggested he drank his coffee black and didn't believe in fun, addressed the room. "Folks, I'm going to need you all to stay put while we take statements."

Cue the collective groan. A few guests shifted uncomfortably, glancing longingly at the door, probably calculating whether they could make a break for it and chastising themselves for not leaving earlier – or coming at all. Nobody dared argue, though. You don't argue with a man in blue with a gun in his holster, whose wiry eyebrows could cut glass.

I stood there, trying to look inconspicuous while my brain replayed the events of the night on an endless loop. The tension between Marissa and Oliver had been so thick you could spread it on toast. And then there was the Prosecco—the very bottle Marissa had poured from, the one that had somehow ended up as the star suspect in this impromptu murder mystery. I stared at the kitchen counter where I'd abandoned my glass, wondering if I'd just dodged death by bubbly.

Oliver sidled up to a small group of guests, attempting what I can only describe as damage control. His tone was calm, his words smooth, but his execution? About as subtle as a middle schooler trying to bluff their way through a book report.

"Best thing we can do now," he said, his tone oddly smooth, "is just... forget what we saw tonight. No need to dwell on unpleasant details, right? Um...poor choice of words. What I mean to say is don't let this effect you." He had the decency to look uncomfortable as if he wasn't a sociopath but just did not have the decorum or finesse necessary to put anyone at ease. "Traumatic for everyone. So sorry you had to witness this. We all feel badly for her." He knew he was digging himself into a hole so he shook his head and just walked away.

What? The words struck me like a slap. Forget what we saw? His casual dismissal seemed almost sinister, as though he were trying to sweep the entire incident under the rug. The guests around him nodded uncertainly, clearly uncertain whether to agree or to challenge his strange advice. I couldn't help but feel a shiver of suspicion. What did Oliver have to gain by downplaying what had happened here? How do you forget a woman dropping dead at a party?

Forget what we saw? What did he think this was, *Men*

in Black? Was he about to flash one of those memory-wiping gizmos? The guests around him nodded awkwardly, clearly unsure if they were supposed to agree or report him to the nearest officer. Meanwhile, I stood there blinking, wondering how he thought anyone could "forget" the sight of a woman foaming at the mouth mid-party.

I glanced around the room, half expecting someone to shout hysterically, *"It was the Prosecco, in the kitchen, with a bone!"* Instead, everyone looked as uneasy as I felt, stealing glances at one another, their faces a mix of suspicion and mild panic.

Then there was Sam, who'd seamlessly transitioned into the role of unofficial host, moving through the room like a well-trained CIA operative. "The bone? Oh, just a deer bone. Totally normal. Coyotes love dragging those around."

Really, Sam? Because if that was a deer bone, then I'm a Rhodes scholar. The thing looked like it had been pulled straight out of a *CSI* episode. And the way he pocketed it with all the subtlety of a magician hiding a rabbit? Yeah, that didn't scream "totally normal" to me.

Sir, bless his clueless little heart, squirmed in my arms, his big puppy eyes silently pleading for a snack or a nap—or possibly both. I scratched his ears, hoping his innocent energy might keep me grounded, because my mind was spinning faster than a politician caught in a scandal.

The police finally started taking statements, working their way around the room like a painfully slow game of musical chairs. When it was my turn, I recounted the night's highlights: the argument between Marissa and Oliver, the bone tug-of-war, and the moment Marissa collapsed. I left out my theory about the Prosecco because, frankly, I wasn't ready to star in my own true-crime docuseries.

Oliver, of course, maintained his "I'm just a simple landlord" routine, his face carefully blank as I spoke. The man was either a master poker player or had completely detached from reality. Either way, his vibe was unnerving.

Eventually, the officers gave us the all-clear to leave, with strict instructions to stay reachable for further questioning. I had maintained my hold on Sir, his warm little body a small comfort against the chilling events of the night, and headed home.

Back at the cabin, I plopped into a chair, Sir padding around the room before curling up on the rug. I was exhausted, bone-tired—literally and figuratively—but my brain wouldn't shut off. Images from the night flickered in my mind like a bad movie: Marissa's collapse, Oliver's strange nonchalance, the Prosecco bottle, and, of course, that damn bone.

Speaking of bones. I glanced at Sir's crate, which he'd apparently turned into a private stash for contraband. Nestled under the blanket was a second bone—shorter than the one he and Pepper had been fighting over but still unsettlingly human-looking. And there, beside it, was a tennis ball.

I pieced it together: Squirt. That sneaky lab must have waltzed into my cabin, dropped off a "welcome to the neighborhood" gift, and pried the door wide open for Sir's great escape. A bone *and* a tennis ball? I sighed, cradling the bone in one hand and the ball in the other – nice gifts for a dog I suppose. Was this bone connected to the one they dropped at the party? From the same skeleton? A deer? I was no forensic expert, but something about this whole situation stunk worse than Sir's puppy breath after eating raw salmon.

"Just deer bones," I muttered to myself, trying to

channel Sam's calm demeanor. But as I stared at the pale, unsettling object in my hand, I couldn't shake the feeling that Legacy Lake was hiding far more than I'd bargained for. And knowing my neighbors might not be a welcome idea.

7

THE HUNKA HUNKA BURNING LOVE GOD

I couldn't sleep; the images of the party and Marissa's haunting me. For hours, I watched Sir sleep, because that's what you do when a tiny, adorable creature invades your home and takes over your heart in under 24 hours. He looked so peaceful, so utterly innocent, I found myself jealous of his ability to snooze through the traumas and existential dread that apparently comes free with adulthood.

Sir stretched out, then curled back into himself, his soft puppy breaths rising and falling like the tide on a calm lake. This was his first week of sleeping in my home, and for the first time, I felt the quiet, undeniable thrill of belonging to someone—or rather, having someone belong to me. I reached out and gently stroked his tiny head, marveling at the warmth of him, the softness of his fur, and the rhythmic rise and fall of his chest.

When his eyelids fluttered open for just a moment—unfocused and adorably groggy—he gave a little sigh, tucked his nose back into his paws, and drifted off again. I eventually lifted him, carefully as if he were made of glass, and placed him in his crate just outside my bedroom door. That's what responsible puppy owners do, right?

As I lay in bed, thoughts and images of the evening swept over me like ocean waves. I couldn't shake the feeling that I'd crossed some invisible line, stepping into a story with an ending I couldn't yet see. I had stumbled into a murder I was sure of it. And my neighbors were all suspects, and to be honest – they probably included me in that category as well.

Just as I finally started to drift off, a sudden noise jolted me upright:

"YAAAAOOOHWOOOO! WHAAARE THE HELL ARE YOU?"

Bang!

I bolted out of bed, heart pounding, as Sir threw himself against the crate door like a battering ram, howling in fear. Half-asleep and wholly panicked, I flung open the door, and Sir launched himself into my arms, whining pitifully before promptly peeing all over me. Because, of course, *that's* what happens when you leave a puppy alone at night. Message received, buddy.

Cursing my rookie mistake—I was supposed to wake him every two to three hours for bathroom breaks—I decided the crate wasn't going to cut it tonight. I spread his blue blanket across my bed, layered it with puppy pee pads, and settled him next to me. He snuggled in immediately, drifting back to sleep as if peeing on me had lifted an emotional weight from his tiny shoulders. Meanwhile, I lay awake, too terrified to move, convinced I'd accidentally roll over and squish him like a pancake.

Around 3 a.m., I decided to sneak him back into the crate. Big mistake. The second I stepped away, Sir let out the saddest, most heart-wrenching whine I'd ever heard. His little paws scratched frantically at the metal door as if I'd exiled him to Siberia, and my guilt skyrocketed. Poor guy—this was his first week away from his mom and littermates, and here I was, abandoning him to the cold, unfeeling prison of crate life.

I caved. Obviously. Scooping him up, I carried him back to bed, where he burrowed into the crook of my arm like a living, breathing teddy bear. His tiny body was warm against mine, and for the first time all night, he seemed completely at peace.

The wind outside picked up, sending pinecones clattering onto the roof, while a lone coyote howled in the distance. I lay there, hand resting protectively on Sir's tiny frame, feeling the steady rhythm of his breathing. But my mind wouldn't rest. *Sir Galahad.* It was a sweet name, sure, but as I whispered it into the darkness, it didn't feel right. It didn't feel *him.*

OUTSIDE, the coyote's cry was picked up by another, and then another, their eerie chorus echoing through the trees, filling the silence with their strange, disembodied voices. The puppy whimpered softly in his sleep, his small paws twitching, and my fingers rested protectively on his fur, feeling the reassuring warmth of him, the steady rise and fall of his breath.

My eyes grew heavy, and the room, dark and expansive, seemed to shift, as if the walls themselves were breathing in time with the night. As sleep pulled me under, I sank into a dream but I was awake — a vision, half-formed and unsettling, appeared:

A man standing in a misty landscape, his figure strong and tall against a backdrop of palm trees and crashing waves. The image emerged more clearly lit from within and outlined by an aura of flickering red that radiated outward as if he were emerging from fire. His eyes dark and glinting like polished stones. Wearing nothing but a loincloth and a fishhook carved from an animal tusk that swung on a tightly woven necklace around his neck, he stood bare chested and bronzed by the sun. Every muscle shone as if chiseled from a dark and sacred wood. His expression one of fierce determination. He looked most definitely like an ancient Hawaiian god – for only a god could have such a perfect body and beautiful face. A hunka, hunka chunka burning love god.

He stood 10 feet away holding a long spear on one hand – not threatening. More like a guardian, a presence neither fully alive nor entirely of this world. After staring at me for a few seconds, he spoke one word, "KOA" – a sound that slammed into me so hard I felt like a huge wave crashed into me, knocked me down and sent me tumbling under water gasping for air before another wave forced me under and rolled me through the foamy water until hitting the shore.

Waiting for me to recover, he continued,

"I am Oumuamua. Koa is your 'aumākua' who will help you bring peace to spirits of many who have not transitioned properly to the afterlife. He is a digger of bones. He will unearth many truths. He will lead you with his eyes and the pointing of his nose. Listen to him. He will protect you."

And with that cryptic message, he turned as if to walk away, hesitating just long enough for me to take along look at the beautiful circular tattoo framing his left buttock. As if he knew I was entranced by this hunka hunka burning man, he turned his gaze back to me and winked then faded away into the glowing mist, leaving me wide-eyed, breathless, and possibly in love (or at least lust) with the ghost of a Hawaiian deity.

I woke with a start, the name Koa resonating in my chest like an echo. The room was cold, the wind howling

55

outside, but Sir was warm against me, his small body rising and falling in steady rhythm.

"Koa," I whispered, testing the name on my tongue. It felt strong, right. A name for someone brave. It was also the initials for Kona, Hawaii's airport and the famous brand of a national camp ground chain.

Morning arrived with soft blue light filtering through the curtains. I slipped out of bed carefully, relieved to find Sir still alive and very much *not* crushed. Thank God he survived the night! It was a sign that I might be able to successfully raise him after all. The vision lingered as I reached for my laptop and typed into the search bar: *What does 'Koa' mean in Hawaiian?*

Brave. Fearless. A warrior. The meaning unfolded on the screen like a sunrise, simple yet profound. *Koa.* It felt raw and primal, a name bursting with strength and virtue, perfectly capturing the spirit I'd sensed in him from the moment he crawled into the crook of my arm. It also carried the essence of the messenger from my dream, or at least similar coloring, the one who had spoken it with such authority.

Still buzzing with curiosity, I typed in the next word from the dream: *'Aumākua.* The results described deceased ancestors who became spiritual guardians, watching over their descendants and influencing their lives. They could appear as animals—sharks, owls, geckos—or as forces of nature, and were honored through prayers, offerings, and chants. It was the kind of thing that felt both sacred and strangely comforting, like discovering a secret handshake between you and the universe.

Then, I searched for the meaning of *'Oumuamua,* the name my dream messenger had given himself. It wasn't a person's name or a god, as I'd first assumed, but a term that meant "a messenger from afar who arrives first." The phrase sent a shiver down my spine. If he was the first to arrive, did that mean more messengers were coming? And if so, what were they bringing—more cryptic guidance, or something else entirely? And if he was the first to arrive – I'd be more than ok if he visited again.

I leaned back, staring at the screen, the gears in my mind turning. *Sir Galahad,* the noble knight of Arthurian legend, suddenly felt as mismatched as a tuxedo at a back-yard barbecue. But *Koa?* That name had fire. It was brave, fearless, and perfect for a puppy who had already shown so much courage. At just nine weeks old, he'd left everything familiar—his mom, his littermates—and faced the unknown with an open heart and wagging tail. A little warrior, playful yet bold.

And that playfulness, I realized, was already starting to draw something out of me. His joy in the simple things—a blanket, a treat, a patch of sunlight—was infectious. It was impossible not to smile when he tumbled after his tail or snuggled up to me with absolute trust. Little did I know then how much his spirited energy would change me: how he'd turn waking up every morning into a gift rather than a bore, how he'd become a magnet for connection, drawing strangers to us like moths to a flame, making it easier for me to meet people. And later, how fiercely protective he'd become when it mattered most.

I reached down and stroked his soft fur, letting my fingers trace the lightning-shaped mark on his tiny frame. It was as if the universe had etched that symbol onto him, a sign of power and purpose. Bending closer, I whispered his new name, my voice barely louder than the morning stillness.

"Good morning, Koa ʻAumākua."

The moment the words left my lips, the air in the room seemed to shift. A current of energy rippled through me, starting at the crown of my head and flowing down my spine. It wasn't a jolt, but a deep, tingling sensation, as if I'd spoken something sacred, something binding. It felt like naming him wasn't just giving him an identity but forging a connection, a protective tether between us that reached deeper than anything I'd ever known.

I watched him stir, his little body curling tighter into his blanket, completely unaware of the gravity of the moment. "Who were you in another life?" I whispered, more to myself than to him.

Koa didn't answer, of course. He just twitched his paws in his sleep, perhaps chasing a dream rabbit or a vision of his own. But as the pale morning light filtered through the windows, I couldn't shake the feeling that this tiny, fearless creature had been sent to me for a reason – and was destined to help me uncover Marissa's murderer.

8

WELCOME TO THE NEIGHBORHOOD

The morning sun was shining, but thankfully not yet blazing hot, and I was trying not to trip over Sir Koa, who had decided that every pothole on the driveway held a personal treasure needing investigation with both nose and mouth. I was just pulling something stringy yucky out of his mouth when I noticed a small group of neighbors casually gathered outside Sam and Brenda's house. They looked like they were having one of those impromptu driveway parties Brenda had mentioned—minus the cocktails and plus an air of gossip so thick you could feel it a mile away. Naturally, I wandered over.

Brenda waved me in like she'd been expecting me. "Kat! Just in time. We're talking about last night."

Of course they were. The wine-tasting-slash-crime-scene was still fresh in everyone's minds. Claire, Ted, and Brenda were leaning against Sam's old red, heavily dented Chevy truck, while a petite blonde with an athletic build and three kids' worth of exhaustion written on her face introduced herself as Jessie, the local realtor. I nodded politely, trying to gauge if she was the type of realtor who would welcome you to a new home with cookies or hand you some hidden fees instead.

"Did you hear?" Brenda asked, her voice low, dramatic. "The official cause of death came back. Marissa died of a heart attack but they also discovered she could have dropped any moment from liver failure."

There was a collective murmur of disbelief.

"Heart attack?" I repeated, skeptically. "I don't know much about hearts and livers, but that looked awfully foamy for organ malfunctions. Honestly, it looked more like poison. Not that I'm an expert. Except, well, I *do* have experience with the topic."

That got their attention. All heads turned toward me; eyebrows raised like I'd just confessed to moonlighting as an assassin. I waved my hand dismissively. "No, no, I don't *use* poison. But I've researched it. In my work buying and selling antiques and oddities, you'd be amazed how many poison-related stories you stumble across. It's fascinating, really.

For example, last year, I acquired what appeared to be an innocent, beautifully carved Victorian teapot. The seller swore it had belonged to her "eccentric great-aunt Ellen," who "never really liked people," but she failed to mention Ellen's unusual hobby: witchcraft of the toxicology spell type.

I didn't find out until later—while sipping tea from it during an online auction preview—that this teapot wasn't just decorative. My tongue went numb halfway through my sales pitch. The bidders were thrilled at the 'live demo,' thinking my increasingly slurred speech was part of a gimmick. It wasn't.

After some quick Googling (and a panicked call to Poison Control), I learned the teapot was laced with a poisonous glaze—a little-known Victorian trend designed to slowly eliminate the competition during tea parties. I mean, who needed networking when you could just outlive your rivals? Fortunately, the potency had declined through the years.

Needless to say, I made it through the ordeal, but the teapot sold for triple the expected price as "The Deadliest Tea Set in London." As for me, I now inspect everything with gloves, a magnifying glass, and occasionally a taster or at least a good laboratory analysis.

"Wait, wait," Jessie interrupted. "Are you saying you think Marissa was *poisoned*?"

I hesitated. "I mean, I don't know for sure. But the foam, the sudden collapse? It doesn't allude to natural causes. And—"

"So, who would poison her?" Claire asked, cutting me off. "I mean, everyone hated Marissa, sure, but that doesn't mean they'd actually *kill* her. We're pretty civilized around here."

"Well, as an unbiased outsider new to everyone, I could offer my observations," I said, suddenly regretting this whole conversation, "Evie and Oliver seem like prime candidates. There was a lot of tension between Marissa and Oliver, and Evie had that weird thing with the lavender spray. Plus, she was acting... odd when she left."

Jessie nodded. "I've always thought Oliver was sketchy. You know, people say his tenants sometimes disappear. There was one who died two doors down from you, Kat. And I know of at least three who mysteriously left in the middle of the night, never to be seen again."

"Wait, what?" I said, looking from face to face. "Is this common knowledge?"

Brenda shrugged. "It's Legacy Lake. We're small-town nosy, but we also know how to keep things... discrete if we like the new tenant...But if we don't like you. Then we really spin a fantastic story to get you to move away."

Her husband shook his head adding quickly, "She is just pulling your leg."

Great. Just what I needed—neighbors who kept their crimes on the down-low and blame the landlord for getting rid of people when in fact, they did it themselves.

Ted chimed in; his voice thoughtful. "But what about what Marissa was eating and drinking? If it *was* poison, it could've been slipped to her food or drink."

The group fell silent, and I suddenly realized all eyes were now on me.

"She was drinking Prosecco," I said cautiously.

"And who brought that?" Jessie asked, her tone sharp as if soliciting a confession from a wayward teenage daughter who snuck off to a party after stealing a bottle from her parent's liquor cabinet.

Oh no. "I, uh... I did," I admitted.

The silence turned icy. Brenda's eyes narrowed just slightly, and Jessie reared her head back like a cat sizing up prey and ready to pounce.

"I didn't poison her!" I blurted. "It was just a normal bottle of Prosecco. I drank it too, remember?"

"Still," Sam said, his voice suspiciously neutral, "you might've slipped something into her glass. Or maybe someone did when you weren't looking. But I didn't see anyone else around her but you."

Fantastic. Now I was a suspect. When in fact I had my own suspicions about Sam and Brenda now – as if they knew where the bodies of Oliver's former tenants were buried and passed their bones off as random deceased deer.

My stomach dropped, and my pulse quickened as I scanned their faces, searching for a glimmer of reassurance. Instead, I found skepticism—polite skepticism, sure, but skepticism nonetheless. The kind where people smile at you like everything's fine while mentally calculating how fast they can alert the authorities. Great. This was turning into *CSI: Legacy Lake,* and I'd somehow become the prime suspect.

I knew one thing for sure: if I ever wanted to make a life here, I'd have to clear my name faster than a toddler with chocolate on their face swears they didn't eat the cake. I couldn't be the weird new neighbor who brought a death bottle to a party. The rumors would spread faster than a wildfire, and suddenly I'd be "that woman" who poisoned Marissa and probably, for good measure, stole Squirt's bone. I opened my mouth to defend myself, but before I could get a word out, Claire stepped forward.

"Hold on, everyone," she said, raising a hand like a traffic cop. "Let's not get carried away. Kat just moved here. She barely knows any of us. Why on earth would she want to poison Marissa? She didn't even know enough to dislike her properly yet!"

Ted nodded solemnly, crossing his arms. "Judge not, lest ye be judged," he said, in his best 'wise elder' voice. "Matthew 7:1."

I blinked, caught off guard by both the defense and the Bible quote. Claire gave me a small, encouraging smile, and Ted's face was filled with calm certainty, like he'd just absolved me from sins I hadn't committed. I wasn't sure how much weight that carried with the group, but it was enough to make the others shift uncomfortably, suddenly unsure of themselves.

Jessie, who had been nibbling on what looked like a protein bar, suddenly chimed in with the confidence of someone who probably closed deals during childbirth. "Look, if we're talking about potential suspects, you need to understand something about Marissa. She made enemies *everywhere*. I mean, brokers, developers, contractors, even the shysters who barely manage to pass as real estate agents —she burned bridges like she had stock in lighter fluid."

Everyone turned to her, clearly intrigued. Jessie leaned against the truck, crossing her arms. "There wasn't a deal she wouldn't strong-arm, a person she wouldn't step over, or a boundary she wouldn't bulldoze. And when it came to Legacy Lake, she wanted it all. The lakefront houses, the hillside developments, even the public access points— Marissa was trying to turn this place into her personal cash cow. And if you didn't play ball? Well, let's just say she didn't bother to play nice."

Brenda raised an eyebrow. "You saying someone finally got sick of her games?"

"I'm saying there's no shortage of people who had *plenty* of reasons to want her to go away," Jessie replied, her voice matter-of-fact. "The only shocking thing about Marissa dying is that it didn't happen sooner. And don't look at me like that," she added, waving her finger in the air and planting one hand on her hip after noting Ted's disapproving expression. "I didn't do it. I'm just saying the woman knew how to rack up a hit list and was probably at the top of everyone's hit list in return."

I shifted uncomfortably, wondering just how many people might have wanted Marissa dead. Suddenly, I didn't feel so much like the prime suspect—I felt more like everyone in Legacy Lake had motive. But only a few had means and opportunity and those few were likely attending the same party. Which would've been comforting, except for the gnawing realization that I had no idea who, if anyone, I could trust.

For the first time since the conversation started, I felt like I wasn't drowning. But if I wanted to stay above water, I'd need to do more than rely on Claire's logic and Ted's scripture. I'd need to find out who actually killed Marissa. Because if there was one thing I'd learned from my antique-dealing days and life in general, it's this: the truth might be hidden, but it always leaves clues and the truth will eventually be revealed.

Trying to deflect the conversation back toward anyone but me, I brought up the bone Koa had unearthed last night. "What about that bone? Any idea where it came from?"

Brenda and Sam exchanged a glance that practically screamed *we know something but aren't telling*.

"It's probably just a deer bone," Sam said, a little too quickly.

Everyone nodded sagely, like they'd just wrapped up a very serious board meeting about murder, and then, one by one, they scattered with vague excuses about getting on with their day, or feeding dogs and kids. It was an exodus fueled less by urgency and more by everyone's desperate need to escape the escalating unease.

I lingered, mostly because I didn't have and plans for the day and partly because Koa had waddled over to a rock ledge near Sam's driveway and made a horrifying discovery. There, resting like some kind of macabre decoration, was the skeletal remains of a deer's lower jaw. Naturally, Koa took one look and thought, *"Snack time!"* He pounced on the thing with the enthusiasm of a toddler discovering an unattended cupcake and started enthusiastically nibbling on the edge of the jaw.

"Koa, no!" I hissed, rushing over, but he just clearly denied he heard me.

Gathering up the puppy, I turned to Sam. "I see what you mean by deer bones."

"We find them in the wood all the time."

"And Squirt?" I asked, raising an eyebrow. "Does he help dig them up? I found a bone and a tennis ball lying outside Koa's crate. It occurred to me that Squirt and maybe Pepper, sprung the puppy loose from crate-prison last night then led him to the party. In fact, where is Squirt? I would have thought you would let him loose in the driveway and hang out with Pepper."

Brenda and Sam froze, their expressions shifting from evasive to downright shocked.

"Sam said you saw him at the party?" Brenda questioned; her voice barely audible.

"Uh... yes?" I said, unsure where this was going.

"That's impossible," Sam said, shaking his head. "Squirt's been dead for years. Only I've ever seen him since he passed. I thought you were messing with me at the party – or that I had hallucinated during the chaos when you pointed at the door and yelled about Squirt."

Oh. Great. A ghost dog. I tried not to look alarmed. Before I knew it, I blurted out, "Well, I *do* see ghosts sometimes. Maybe I've just got a thing for paranormal stuff. Occupational hazard when you spend your life digging up oddities with questionable histories."

"Fascinating," Brenda said, cocking her head as if intrigued by my paranormal powers and embracing the reality of my unreality.

Before the conversation could get any weirder, Koa wiggled like he had to pee so I let him go, and he took off, scrambling down into Brenda's side yard like he owned the place. I followed, calling his name, only to discover something surprising: a small patch of cannabis plants growing in a well-hidden garden among thriving culinary herbs.

Brenda followed, her tone casual as she explained, "I use them to make canna-butter and bake cookies. My friend's going through chemo, and it helps with her nausea. And, you know, sometimes I bake cookies for myself. Glaucoma. Helps Sam sleep as well."

I raised an eyebrow. "Organic, I hope?"

Brenda grinned. "Always. Wait a minute before you go. I have something for you."

Brenda disappeared into the house and returned a moment later with a small baggie.

"Peanut butter cookies," she said, handing it to me with a sly smile. "Welcome to the neighborhood. They're a bit strong, so maybe start with half."

Nothing says *welcome to the neighborhood* like a baggie of cookies.

9

LAVENDER AND MUSHROOMS

That evening, I found myself curled up on Maggie's oversized couch, nursing a cup of tea that tasted vaguely like twigs with a hint of peppermint. Maggie, ever the picture of holistic health, sat across from me with the kind of serene expression that only comes from years of yoga, herbal tinctures, and the ability to remain calm while wrestling a rabid Labrador in her veterinary office. Her Portuguese Water Dog, Sunshine, sprawled out on the rug like she owned the place, her head resting on a squeaky toy shaped like a block of tofu. Koa, on the other hand, was zooming around like he'd just discovered caffeine, occasionally stopping to stare at Sunshine as if trying to figure out how to get it away from her.

"I just don't know if this place is right for me," I confessed, staring into my tea like it held the answers to my existential crisis. "First, there's a death at a wine party. Then there are neighbors who are sweet but act like they've buried secrets — literally. And Koa keeps digging up things that may or may not be deer bones, and frankly, I'm afraid to ask.

And then there's Oliver, whose aw-shucks demeanor

barely covers a terrifying lack of empathy, and Brenda and Sam, who seem allergic to answering direct questions about bones. Oh, and let's not forget Evie's glove stunt. What's she doing skulking around Oliver's porch with gardening gloves? Plotting her next lavender attack?"

Maggie nodded sympathetically. "That was hilarious - Evie spraying lavender hydrosol like its pepper spray, but it wasn't malicious. Every neighborhood has its oddballs—most are lovable, and a few are best kept at arm's length. Legacy Lake is your typical abnormally normal All-American community."

Maggie leaned forward, lowering her voice conspiratorially. "Speaking of strange things... I heard from my neighbor —an ER nurse—about Marissa's autopsy."

I set my mug down. "Oh? Do tell."

"They found traces of toxins like *convallatoxin,* a cardiac glycoside given to heart patients but also known as a plant toxin that dogs can get into if they eat certain plants like Lily of the Valley plants and especially their berries. Which reminds me – don't let your dog nibble on plants and especially red, sweet berries except for raspberries. Lots of things may be toxic, but you really only have to avoid feeding him onions, chocolate, and grapes...I'll give you a list for your dog later but really interesting thing is this -they also found what could have killed her - *Amanita bisporigera.* The 'Destroying Angel.' It's one of the deadliest mushrooms in the world," Maggie said, sitting back as casually as if she were discussing a new recipe.

I blinked at her. "Destroying Angel? That sounds like a goth metal band, not a fungus. How did it get in her system? Salad? Soup? A poorly thought-out charcuterie board? Or... oh my God...the mushroom canapes."

"They don't know yet," Maggie shrugged. "It's not enough to definitively say it killed her, but it's suspicious, don't you think? Poison mushrooms don't exactly scream 'natural causes.'"

I mulled it over while Koa attempted to chew Sunshine's tail and got a royal growl in return. "It definitely explains the foam," I muttered, mostly to myself. "But it also makes me wonder — who'd use a mushroom? Takes some advanced level knowledge about toxicity."

Before Maggie could answer, her husband John walked in, looking like he'd just stepped out of an L.L.Bean catalog — rugged, handsome, and quaintly wholesome in a you-can-depend-on-me kinda way. He gave me a warm smile. "Hey, Kat. I'm taking Sunshine and Koa for their first pack walk. Be back in 30."

"Pack walk?" I asked, watching as he deftly clipped a leash onto Sunshine's collar.

"Yeah," Maggie said, her tone light. "A few of the neighbors take their dogs out together and walk the circle surrounding the huge greenspace outside our back yards every evening. We can watch them from the upper deck. It's a thing."

Of course it was a thing. Gossip and rumors go round and round in this community and I was beginning to understand where dogs fit into the picture – pack and yack walks. I nodded, letting John whisk Koa away, and turned back to Maggie.

"So, about these neighbors of yours," I said, bringing her back to the real gossip.

Maggie settled in. "Well, Marissa didn't exactly win 'most popular.' People on the ridge are still fuming over the shoddy work on her developments. Cracked foundations, leaky basements, terrible HOA fees that seem to rise as frequently as Elon Musk's Starlink satellites—you name it. And she made a lot of enemies. Oliver and Evie couldn't stand her. Jess lost deals to her shady tactics, and Sam hated her plans to bulldoze the old homestead for a development. And that's just the shortlist."

"Sounds like everyone had a motive," I said, half-joking. "And how does everyone seem to know each other? I thought there were Lakers – those who actually live on the shoreline – and Lookers - those who lived on the ridge overlooking the lake?

Maggie nodded. "Not a huge community! And everyone is either looking up or looking down on people around here comparing themselves to one another. Did you know Oliver's sister designed Marissa's garden? And Marissa's house is just down the street from me. It's practically a botanical masterpiece. If Marissa had a friend, it would've been her."

I filed that away for later as Maggie asked if I wanted something stronger than tea and went into the kitchen to pour us near full glasses of rose. Maggies calming lavender diffuser playing a soft melody in the background had already worked its magic and I felt relaxed for the first time since witnessing Marissa's death.

Handing me a glass of wine that felt like a lifeline, she asked, "How is it going with Koa?" before settling into an easy chair across from me like a therapist who specializes in the human-animal bond. Kind of like marriage therapy focusing on communication and bonding except your partner shouts little yips in the background rather than grunts and shrugs.

"I have to confess I'm losing my mind. Koa is outsmarting me at every turn."

She smiled knowingly. "Puppy chaos, huh? Welcome to the new puppy motherhood. Tell me—what's he done?"

"The potty bell," I groaned, gesturing dramatically. "He rings it for *everything*. To go outside, to get attention, to troll me because he can. I swear, he thinks it's the greatest toy ever invented."

Maggie laughed, a full, hearty laugh that made Sunshine's tail thump against the rug. "Of course, he does! Kat, the potty bell isn't just for Koa—it's for you. Training a puppy is really about training the *owner*. Puppies are tiny geniuses at manipulating humans."

I blinked at her. "So what you're saying is, my dog is Pavlov, and I'm the salivating experiment."

"Exactly," Maggie said with a grin. "Every time you jump up when he rings the bell, you're reinforcing his behavior. He's learning that if he wants you to spring into action, all he has to do is ring the magic noise-maker. Classic puppy power move."

I slumped further into the couch, defeated. "Great. I've been outsmarted by a creature who thinks his tail is a chew toy."

Maggie leaned forward, her voice turning slightly more serious. "Okay, here's what you do. First, you have to teach Koa that the bell only works for actual potty breaks. If he rings it just to mess with you, ignore him. It'll drive him crazy for a bit, but eventually, he'll figure it out."

"You mean ignore the incessant ringing? That's like asking me to ignore a toddler banging pots and pans together."

"You're going to need more wine," Maggie deadpanned, "Lots of wine." Taking a sip of hers for emphasis.

"Already tried that," I said. "Turns out wine doesn't drown out the sound of jingling bells or soothe my bruised ego."

Maggie chuckled. "You've got to be consistent. Boundaries are key."

"Boundaries," I muttered. "Got it. What about the midnight wake-ups? He doesn't even bark—he just stares at me like some kind of Chucky the creepy doll dog until I wake up. It's like living in a horror movie."

"Oh, Sunshine did that too when she was a puppy," Maggie said, shaking her head. "It's their way of saying, 'Hey, human, pat attention to me'. The trick is to make midnight potty breaks as boring as possible. No talking, no playing, just business. Take him out, let him do his thing, and back to bed. Make it so dull that he decides waking you up isn't worth it."

"Dull?" I scoffed. "This is the same dog who went out to pee and heard a squirrel at 3 a.m. and zoomed all over the yard like his life depended on eradicating it while I tried for what seemed like an hour to capture him – stark naked except for flip flops, I might add. It's too hot to sleep in pajamas."

Maggie laughed so hard, she nearly spilled her wine. Sunshine raised her head, giving her mom a judgmental side-eye before flopping back down.

"Okay, fair," Maggie admitted. "Koa's high-energy. But that just means you've got to outsmart him. And redirect him."

"Oh, don't even get me started on the chewing phase," I said, shaking my head. "If it's not nailed down, he chews it. Shoes, furniture, my socks—especially my socks. He's obsessed."

"Of course, he is," Maggie said, nodding sagely. "Socks smell like you. To a puppy, that's basically the best thing ever. But you've got to redirect him to something he *can* chew. Get some good chew toys and make them irresistible. Peanut butter works wonders. Smear a little on a toy, and he'll forget all about your socks."

"Peanut butter," I repeated. "Why does that sound like a bribe?"

"Because it is," Maggie said with a smirk. "Training a puppy is 90% bribery, 10% patience."

I took a long sip of wine. "I feel like I'm failing. I'm sleep-deprived, and I haven't had a moment of peace since he showed up."

"You're not failing," Maggie said firmly. "Every puppy parent feels like that in the beginning. You're doing great. Puppies are chaos, but they're also pure joy. Trust me, it gets easier."

I arched an eyebrow. "Define 'easier.'"

"You'll sleep through the night again. Eventually," Maggie said, trying to suppress a grin. "And Koa will stop chewing socks. If you put them away."

"Comforting," I said dryly.

"Kat," Maggie said, her voice softening, "puppy training is about building trust and a bond that lasts a lifetime. These early weeks are tough, but they're also the foundation for everything else. And you're not alone. I'm here to help. You've got this."

Despite the exhaustion and chaos, I couldn't help but smile.

"Thanks, Maggie," I said. "I needed that."

"Anytime," Maggie said, raising her coffee mug. "Here's to surviving puppyhood—and maybe even enjoying it."

"Cheers to that," I said, raising my glass.

Eventually, John returned with Koa, who bounded in like he'd discovered treasure. I scooped him up and noticed something stuck to his fur.

"What's this?" I asked, peeling off what looked like a paper label.

John leaned over. "That's a hydrosol label from Sandra's lavender farm. Koa must've picked it up when he ran through the open gate at Marissa's house. Looks like the investigators forgot to latch it."

A question emerged from my wine-hazed mind that unsettled me. Why did Sandra's lavender farm keep cropping up?

Koa, ever the fast learner, realized Sunshine wasn't going to share her toys readily, had taken possession of another one of Sunshine's toys and was now parading it around the living room like he'd won the lottery.

I stood up to take it from her when I heard Sunshine's low growl of disapproval but Maggie encouraged me to just let Koa take it home. Better to chew on than my socks.

Maggie handed me a small bottle of lavender essential oil and a diffuser as I got ready to leave. "Here," she said with a wink. "Lavender helps with anxiety. Just don't spray it at people unless absolutely necessary."

I laughed, clutching the bottle like it was some kind of talisman. If Legacy Lake was this weird after just one month, I was going to need all the calming scents I could get.

10

DRIVEWAY DETECTIVES
PARTY TEAM

It's been a week since the party and the neighborhood was still buzzing – especially since the new intel about Death Angels swept through the community despite the nurse breaking HIPAA confidentiality laws and the police keeping silent.

In the tradition of all great driveway detectives, the neighbors got to work in earnest: with lawn chairs, a mismatched assortment of snacks, and a lot of wine. They reconvened in Sam and Brenda's driveway, their impromptu meeting place of choice, to do what they did best—gossip. It didn't matter that the coroner had officially ruled Marissa's death as liver failure caused by years of heavy drinking. No one was buying it. Not for a second.

I walked up with Koa, just in time to hear Jess, the petite and perpetually polished realtor. She leaned forward in her chair, eyes gleaming with a mixture of determination and too much rosé. "I'm telling you, it was *Evie*. Who else has the knowledge, the means, and—let's face it—the sheer audacity to pull something like this off?"

Brenda raised an eyebrow. "You're saying Evie poisoned

Marissa? With what, her lavender spray? Maybe she gave her an overdose of soothing vibes."

"No," Jess said, with the air of someone about to drop a bombshell. "With a *mushroom*. Specifically, the 'destroying angel.' I heard one of the ER nurses read the toxicology report"

The group collectively leaned in; the way people do when they want to look cool but are actually dying to hear more.

"Think about it," Jess continued, warming to her theory. "Evie knows all about plants and fungi. She's always out there, foraging and lecturing people on what's edible and what's deadly. Remember that hiking group she led last year? She spent *half an hour* talking about the exact symptoms of eating poisonous mushrooms. She even handed out little laminated guides!"

"That's true," Brenda admitted, sipping her champagne. "She had an unnerving amount of detail. She even mentioned the timeframes. Like, with the destroying angel, you don't feel the effects for five hours after you eat it. If Marissa was poisoned, it had to have happened *before* the party."

"That tracks with the toxicology report," I chimed in, trying to sound more confident than I felt. "The coroner found traces of the destroying angel in her system. Not enough to outright kill her right away, but combined with her, uh... 'well-loved' liver, it's no wonder she didn't make it through the night."

Jess clapped her hands. "Exactly! And who better to slip her a deadly mushroom than someone who knows exactly how they work? I'm telling you, Evie did it. She has the knowledge, she has the motive—Marissa was trying to buy her property, remember? And she has the... what's the word?"

"Creepy factor?" Ted offered.

"Exactly," Jess agreed.

Brenda looked thoughtful. "A friend of mine mentioned something interesting the other day. She said Evie got sick after the party but recovered pretty quickly. If she handled the mushrooms without ingesting them, that could explain it. You know, just enough exposure to make her feel awful but not enough to do real damage."

"Wait," I said, holding up a hand. "What about the glove? I found one outside Oliver's house before the party, and the matching glove was sticking out of Evie's pocket when she was arguing with Marissa. What if it had traces of the mushroom on it? And that's what made her sick?"

The group fell silent, the implications settling over us like a fog.

"Evie did look pretty guilty when Oliver told her to grab the glove," I added. "She practically sprinted away."

"But how would she have gotten the mushrooms into Marissa's system before the party?" Brenda mused.

Jess shrugged. "Maybe she sent over a peace offering. Like, 'Hey, sorry I don't want to sell my house to you. Here's a nice mushroom risotto.'"

Claire weighed in. "If that's how Evie makes peace, remind me never to tick her off."

Ted, ever the moral compass of the group, cleared his throat. "Now, let's not jump to conclusions. Innocent until proven guilty. And lots of suspects to consider from what I hear on the golf course - lots of people hated her."

Jess rolled her eyes. "Ted, we're not jumping. We're theorizing. It's *different*."

"Sure it is," Ted muttered, taking a swig from a Canadian Molson beer.

I leaned back in my chair, letting the theories swirl around me. It was all plausible—Evie's knowledge, her motive, the mysterious glove—but something didn't sit right. Maybe it was too convenient. Maybe it was the wine. Or maybe it was the fact that the more I learned about Legacy Lake, the more I realized *everyone* here had a motive to want Marissa gone.

As the group toasted to their growing "Evie did it" theory, I couldn't help but feel a pang of doubt. Solving this was going to take more than wine-fueled speculation. And I wasn't about to let myself get swept up in the tide of driveway detectives, judges and executioners without digging deeper.

For now, though, I was glad they were no longer focused on me and my Prosecco – although that could change. I raised my glass with the rest of them, clinking it against Brenda's with a faint smile. After all, if I'd learned one thing about this town, it was this: nothing brings neighbors together like a little scandal and a lot of wine.

11

LEGACIES AND LOTS

It was supposed to be a peaceful morning walk, the kind where I could breathe in the crisp lake air, let Koa burn off some of his endless energy, and maybe pretend for five minutes that I wasn't living in the middle of a small-town murder mystery. But, as usual, Koa had other plans.

I was mid-sip from my travel mug of coffee when Koa, unleashed and unrepentant, dashed toward a patch of dirt near Oliver's house, his little nose twitching with purpose. "Koa, no!" I called, but he was already in full excavation mode, dirt flying behind him like he was auditioning for *Gold Rush: Puppy Edition.*

And then, there it was. Another bone.

I froze, my coffee suddenly tasting like regret. The thing was long, unnervingly white, and unmistakably *not* a stick. Koa wagged his tail proudly, the bone clamped between his jaws.

"Koa, drop it," I said, my voice a little higher than normal. He responded by prancing in circles, bone held high like a banner of victory. I managed to grab him, wrestle the bone free, and tried very hard not to think about the fact that it looked disturbingly... human.

That's when Sam appeared, ambling down the road with the kind of deliberate nonchalance pretending, *I was just out for a walk. I definitely wasn't spying on you.*

"Oh, hey there, Kat," he said, a little too cheerfully. "Looks like Koa's at it again, huh? Bone-collecting sleuth, that one." He let out a nervous chuckle, his eyes darting to the dirt patch Koa had been digging in.

I held up the bone. "Sam, please tell me this is just from a deer or a very unlucky cow."

"Deer, definitely deer," he said quickly, nodding like a bobblehead. "Happens all the time around here. You know, animals die, nature does its thing, yadda yadda..." His voice trailed off, and for a moment, his eyes shifted, almost imperceptibly, to the hillside behind Oliver's house.

My curiosity ignited like a Fourth of July sparkler. "Sam, is there something you're not telling me?"

He hesitated, rubbing the back of his neck. "Well... there *are* rumors. About unmarked pioneer graves in the area. Nothing official, of course. Just, uh, local lore."

"Local lore?" I raised an eyebrow, crossing my arms. "This is the second bone Koa's found. Are you saying there's a possibility these are *human* bones?"

Before he could answer, Brenda, who had been power-walking with hiking sticks half-jogged down the spur road towards us. "Oh, for heaven's sake, Sam, just tell her."

Sam groaned. "Brenda, come on—"

"No, I'm done with the secrets," she said, her hands on her hips. "The graveyard's on our land, Kat. Up on the hillside. It's been there for generations, and Marissa was trying to buy up properties all around the lake, including ours. She snapped up a lot on one side of ours and we had to hustle to snap up the lot on the other side. She didn't care about the history. All she wanted was to bulldoze it for high-end vacation homes."

My jaw dropped. "You're saying Marissa's plans could've disturbed actual pioneer graves? Why didn't you tell anyone?"

Sam sighed, his shoulders slumping. "Because if word got out, the land could be seized, turned into a historical site, or worse, torn up by investigators who surmise they were bodies buried by a recent serial killer. There are even developers who uncover bones while they are building, ignore them and build right over them despite the laws. Then come the lawyers looking for anything they could litigate over. My family's kept it quiet for decades. We thought we were protecting it."

"And Marissa was threatening all of that," I said softly, the puzzle pieces clicking together in my mind.

"Exactly," Brenda said, her voice tight. "And she didn't care who she had to bulldoze—living or dead—to get what she wanted."

I glanced at Sam, who looked like he'd aged ten years in ten minutes. "Sam," I said carefully, "you didn't... I mean, you wouldn't..."

His eyes widened. "What? No! Kat, come on, you know me. I might've hated Marissa's plans, but I'd never—" He stopped himself, looking almost wounded by the suggestion. "I swear, Kat. It wasn't me."

I wanted to believe him. I *did* believe him. But the problem with Legacy Lake was that everyone seemed to have both a motive and a secret.

I forced a smile. "Okay. I believe you. But if it wasn't you..."

"It's either Oliver or Evie," Brenda cut in, her voice sharp.

Sam muttered something under his breath that sounded like, "Or maybe Prosecco."

Again, with me as a suspect. But Evie had the knowledge. Both Evie and Oliver had motive, means and opportunity. But there were too many questions still unanswered. Why the glove? Why mushrooms? Maybe – just maybe – they were in on it together. Or Sam killed her to keep her from wrestling his land away from him and preserving his graveyard. Conveniently up the hillside from Oliver – who has had tenants mysteriously disappear. Were Sam and Oliver somehow in cahoots? Or all three?

Koa squirmed out of my grasp, dashing off toward another dirt patch. "No, Koa, not again!" I shouted, chasing after him.

Sam and Brenda watched me go, their expressions a mix of concern and something else—something I couldn't quite put my finger on. But as I wrestled Koa back onto his leash, one thing was clear.

If I wanted to clear the air—and my name—I was going to have to check out the suspects myself and start with a visit with Evie.

12

DESTROYING ANGELS

The gravel crunched underfoot as I made my way up the winding path to Evie's house, tucked into the edge of the ponderosa pine forest like something out of a fairytale, that seemed peaceful at first glance. Huge pots of English Garden wildflowers stood sentinel in the front yard, their blooms catching the morning sun, and several herb boxes lined the porch, filled with fragrant rosemary, thyme, and lavender. But the aura of serenity didn't fool me. I had questions, and Evie, with her deep knowledge of plants and fungi, might have answers.

Spotting a sign with an arrow that pointed to a small cottage office and read "Evie's Herbal Apothecary", I veered to the right and wandered down a short path that led to a vibrant red door.

I knocked lightly, hoping I didn't look as suspicious as I felt. After a moment, the door swung open, revealing Evie, her earthy, serene demeanor somehow offset by the random hairs springing loose from bun atop her head held in place with a chopstick. She wore a sundress that looked as though it had been handwoven from tie-dyed moonlight and good vibes. She was ageless. I couldn't tell is she was in her 40s or an old soul who discovered the fountain of youth like a vampiress who was actually more than 100 years old.

"Kat!" she said warmly, her face lighting up with a genuine smile. "What a lovely surprise. Come in, come in."

The cottage smelled of lavender and something else—an earthy, musky aroma that made me think of damp forests after rain. The walls were lined with shelves overflowing with books, jars of dried herbs, and small bottles labeled with names like *Calendula Tincture* and *Echinacea Extract*. Dried bundles of flowers hung from the ceiling, giving the whole place the vibe of an apothecary run by a woodland fairy.

"Thanks, Evie," I said, stepping inside and taking in the eclectic space. "I was hoping you might be able to give me some tips on foraging. I figured if anyone knows their way around the local flora and fungi, it's you."

Evie's face lit up with delight. "Oh, you're getting into foraging! That's wonderful. Lots of medicinal herbs nearby and fall mushrooms will pop up in a few weeks. Mushrooms are such fascinating little beings, aren't they? They're like the healers of the forest. Did you know they can detoxify soil, connect trees through underground networks, and even be used in medicine? Truly magical."

I nodded, filing away her enthusiasm for future analysis. "Yeah, I thought it might be a fun hobby, especially now that I'm spending more time outside with Koa. But I want to make sure I know what I'm doing. Don't want my dog to accidentally eat something poisonous."

"Smart," she said, motioning for me to sit at her kitchen table, which was covered in an assortment of jars, tea mugs, and a half-finished knitting project. "You have such a cute dog. Added a little life to the party – pun intended, she winked. "So, what are you hoping to find? Chanterelles? Morels? They're coming into season soon."

"That sounds great," I said, sitting down. "But I'm also curious about the ones to avoid. You know, just in case I come across something dangerous."

Evie poured us each a cup of tea from a pot already steeping on the counter. "There are definitely a few you need to watch out for," she said, settling across from me. Instantly letting me know that she knew I had heard about the toxicology report, she continued. "Destroying angels, for one. They're beautiful but absolutely lethal. One bite could be fatal if you don't get treatment in time."

"Destroying angels," I repeated, trying to keep my voice casual. "Those are the ones that look like little white parasols, right?"

"Exactly," Evie said, her eyes lighting up. "Pure white, often found near hardwood trees. They're tricky because they look similar to edible mushrooms like puffballs when they're young. But once they mature, they're unmistakable." She sipped her tea thoughtfully. "I've only come across them a few times, but I make a point to teach people about them. Knowledge is the best protection."

Her enthusiasm was disarming. For someone who might have had a hand in Marissa's untimely demise, she certainly didn't give off a murderous vibe. If anything, she seemed deeply committed to helping people avoid harm. My gaze drifted to a book lying open on the counter behind her. The title, *Deadly Flora: A Guide to Poisonous Plants and Fungi*, practically screamed for attention.

"Mind if I take a look at that?" I asked, gesturing to the book.

"Oh, sure," she said, her smile faltering slightly as she followed my gaze.

I flipped through the pages, pausing at the section on destroying angels. The glossy photo of the pure white mushroom looked almost serene, but the accompanying text painted a grim picture: *Extremely toxic. Ingestion can lead to liver failure and death. Symptoms often delayed for hours, making treatment difficult.*

"Scary stuff," I murmured, glancing up at Evie. "Do you think it's a good idea to wear gloves when handling mushrooms like this?"

Evie leaned back in her chair, cradling her tea mug in both hands. "Gloves can be helpful if you're handling something you want to identify but aren't planning to eat. I usually wear them for gardening or harvesting, especially in cold or wet weather. But for mushrooms I know well? I don't bother. Familiarity breeds confidence."

"What kind of gloves do you recommend I take along on foraging walks?" I asked, feigning casual interest.

"I always use Black Diamond gloves with wrist leashes," she said. "They're sturdy and perfect for serious work. Definitely not the flimsy cotton kind you see at hardware stores."

"So, you wouldn't take a pair of regular cotton gardening gloves?" I pressed.

Evie laughed, a light, airy sound. "Oh, hell no. Those are useless for anything practical. But funny you mention gloves—I ended up taking home a pair from Oliver's party. He thought they were mine, but they weren't. I was so shook up about Marissa's death, I didn't stop to think. I just stuffed them in my bag. I think they're still in my shed somewhere. They must belong to Sandra. She wears them even if she is just cutting flowers in her yard. Have no idea why Oliver thought they were mine instead of Sandra's. He is so oblivious and disconnected from people sometimes I wonder if he is on the spectrum."

Interesting. I decided not to press the matter further for now. Instead, I steered the conversation back to her background. "You seem to know so much about plants and mushrooms. How did you get into all this?"

Evie's face softened, and a wistful smile played at her lips. "It started when I was a kid. My grandmother was an herbalist, and she used to take me on long walks through the woods, teaching me about the plants and their uses. She believed that the earth provides everything we need to heal ourselves—if we know where to look. I guess that stuck with me."

"That's amazing," I said, genuinely intrigued. "So, you've always been focused on healing?"

"Absolutely," she said, her eyes brightening. "I am a healer. I'm a firm believer in natural remedies supporting our body's ability to heal itself. Modern medicine has its place, of course, but there's something so empowering about being able to heal yourself with what nature provides. I've seen it change lives—people recovering from chronic pain, anxiety, even grief—with the right herbs and a little guidance."

Her passion was undeniable, and for a moment, I found myself warming to her. But then I remembered Marissa and the mysterious circumstances surrounding her death. I couldn't ignore the fact that Evie's deep knowledge of plants and fungi could also be used for less noble purposes.

"Do you ever worry about people misusing this knowledge?" I asked.

"Sometimes," she admitted, her expression growing serious. "That's why I'm careful about who I teach. Most people just want to learn how to make a good herbal tea mix or salve for a bug bite. But there's always the potential for harm if the wrong person gets their hands on something dangerous. It's a fine line."

I nodded, her words only deepening my suspicion about who she taught and who was in on the last mushroom identifying walk when she handed out those laminated cards and talked about Death Angels.

Evie looked sadly around the room, her voice dropping as she said, "Poor Marissa. Misguided but not evil. She did not deserve to die by a toxic mushroom as I've heard was in the tox report. I had seen her earlier in the day before the party.

"I do stop by occasionally to pick up hydrosols from Sandra. She's got the best lavender distillery in the area. In fact, Marissa was just leaving when I arrived. I think she was picking up some lavender products as well."

My ears perked up. "You saw Marissa that day?"

"Yes," she said, her tone casual. "We didn't speak, but she looked... preoccupied. I assumed it was just Marissa being Marissa."

I nodded, filing the detail away for later. "Do you mind if I borrow this book?" I asked, holding up *Deadly Flora*.

"Not at all," Evie said, her smile returning. "It's always good to be informed. Just be careful—it's not exactly light bedtime reading. Come to think of it, a good puppy momma should learn a bit about what kinds of common plants are potentially toxic and even fatal to dogs."

"Fatal to dogs?" Between my conversation with Maggie and Evie, it was beginning to dawn on me that I shouldn't let Koa just sniff and nibble his way around the neighborhood. "Oh my god! What should I be on the lookout for?"

"Not much around here. Watch out for foxtails. Make sure to pull them out of his paws after you walk because they can burrow in cause a lot of pain – and they get in ears and it's a bigger to get them out. Vets usually have to sedate the dog to pull it out. You'll know if your dog gets one imbedded. He will hold up his paw or shake his hear like he has a terrible earache."

I was beginning to think I would never let him out of

the house again. But she pointed to the book in my hand and talked about not worrying. not too many poisonous plants and berries around unless they are ornamentals in someone's private garden.

Feeling slightly less paranoid about how many ways my puppy could die if I didn't watch him like a hawk, I slipped the book into my bag and stood to leave. "Thanks for the tea and the tips, Evie. I'll let you know how my foraging adventures go."

"Anytime," she said, walking me to the door. "And if you ever want to join me on a foraging trip, just say the word. I'd be glad to teach you."

As I walked back to the cabin, my mind buzzed with questions. Evie's warmth and passion for healing were genuine, but there was something about her demeanor that didn't sit right. The gloves, the book, her casual mention of seeing Marissa that day – a good 5 hours before the party— it all felt connected, but the pieces weren't lining up just yet.

"Looks like we've got some reading to do," I muttered to Koa, as I walked in the door and released him from his crate.

That evening, I opened the book and started flipping through the pages, determined to uncover what I should keep Koa away from and gain some insights into poisonous plants.

I flipped to the section on Destroying Angels first.

JUST ON A WHIM, I looked up toxic ornamental plants people grow that I should also keep Koa away from. Not likely he would nibble on roses given the thorn issue although I have seen him lift a leg precariously close to protruding thorns in Claires rose garden during our driveway party. Flipping the pages I saw photos of Foxglove

– and pausing to reflect realized they were not around here. My hillside sported brilliant blue Iris and that was a different story – ah toxic to cats but not necessarily dogs, according to the book. Passing several other photos that I hadn't recalled seeing in the neighborhood, I noticed a very pretty Lily of the Valley.

Known as Lady's Tears, it's said to have first bloomed where Eve's tears fell as she left the Garden of Eden. Its flowering season is from May to June, producing pure white, highly-fragrant bell-shaped blooms that droop over like lady's tears. The flowers become deep red berries that taste sweet to children who have been known to die from eating them. Both the flower and the berry add interest to the contrasting dark green stem and are often used in flower arrangements. All parts of the plant, especially the roots, are poisonous. Just 1-5 berries could kill a person.

PRETTY DEADLY BUT out of season apparently. And I hadn't seen any around the neighborhood – too hot. But then again, I haven't really known what to look for. Perhaps I should take Evie up on her offer of a private flora expedition.

Whether Evie was a healer, a killer, or something in between, I was going to find out eventually – but there were other suspects yet to question.

13

PAWS TO THE CAUSE

It started as one of those days that could have been peaceful —if I didn't live in a place where mysteries were as abundant as pinecones. The day began with Koa staring at me expectantly, tail wagging like a metronome set to "high anxiety." I could tell he wanted a walk, or maybe he just wanted to sniff every blade of grass in Legacy Lake for clues to crimes no one was asking him to solve. So, I took him up the stairs to our driveway that stretched like a pinky finger off the spur road connecting me to my neighbors.

My head was spinning from the tangle of secrets I'd been unraveling, and frankly, I wasn't sure what to do with the mounting evidence pointing toward Evie, Oliver, or both. Should I go to the police? Was I even ready to make that leap?

Before I could gather my thoughts and make a decision, I saw Oliver gimping along towards me. I frowned. He just appeared uninvited like an overly nosy landlord for the second time. Clearly, I was going to have to set a boundary with him.

Oliver, even under the best of circumstances, had a way about him that made me think "local troll masquerading as a human." With his perpetually hunched posture, wild shock of white hair that seemed to defy both gravity and reason, and the odd, shambling gait of someone who was one mismatched sock away from tripping over his own feet, he could have walked straight out of a fairy tale about bridge-dwelling trolls. His skin had the pallor of someone who spent most of his life indoors, but his knotted hands and thick, stubby fingers hinted at a lifetime of hard labor—or possibly throttling his enemies in a crumbling stone cave and tossing them into a "pioneer graveyard".

Even his voice contributed to the image. When Oliver spoke, it was a high-pitched oh-golly, punctuated by sudden bursts of energy that made you wonder if he was about to tell you the location of buried treasure or curse you for stepping on his property. His attempted laugh, never quite developed, was a wheezing, thumping fake chuckle that sounded like it came from deep within a hollow log.

His wardrobe didn't help. Today, he was wearing his usual getup: khakis that were at least a size too big and cinched with a belt that looked like it might double as a weapon, a plaid button-down that had seen more than one decade, and a pair of scuffed loafers that somehow managed to look both too small and too large at the same time. All of it added to his air of "the outcast who got banished from his forest kingdom for mismanaging the treasure hoard and relegated to living under a bridge harassing passersby."

"Kat!" he exclaimed, spreading his arms as if we were old friends as he took a step backward. "I wanted to drop by and, uh, apologize for that unfortunate wine-tasting event. Really not the kind of welcome I intended for you. Shocking, horrible, wasn't it? I would have dropped by sooner but I've been a little under the weather since the party."

I plastered on a polite smile, suppressing the urge to roll my eyes. "Oliver, I appreciate the apology, but may I suggest something? In the future, maybe call first before dropping by. It's just... well, it's polite."

His face reddened slightly, and he adopted that "aw shucks" expression he wore like a second skin. "Oh, sure, sure! Didn't mean to intrude. I just figured, you know, since I'm your landlord and all..."

I raised an eyebrow. "Remember, being my landlord doesn't give you the right to show up unannounced."

"Of course, of course!" he said quickly, backing up a step. "You're absolutely right. I'll call next time."

I nodded, satisfied, but I wasn't about to let him leave without asking a few questions. "Oliver, about the party... I couldn't help but notice the tension between you and Marissa. What was that about?"

He waved a hand dismissively. "Oh, that? Marissa was just being Marissa—jealous and petty. She wanted to buy my properties, but I wouldn't sell. She hated that."

"She seemed pretty determined," I said, watching his face carefully. "Why not sell? You've got a lot of properties, don't you?"

Oliver hesitated, and for a brief moment, his easygoing façade cracked. "It's not just about the money," he said, his voice tightening. "Sandra—my sister—she's always on my case about it. Wants me to sell everything, including the cabin you're in, so she can cash out her share. Says I'm 'cash poor and real estate rich.'"

"She owns part of the properties?" I asked, surprised.

"Oh, half of everything," Oliver admitted, his tone souring. "Our parents left the estate to both of us, but Sandra's more... practical. She wants to sell the lavender farm, focus on her precious garden, and move on with her life. But I'm not ready to let go of the lake houses. They've been in the family for generations. She doesn't get it."

Oliver snapped, his polite veneer slipping. "Thinks I'm

some kind of anchor weighing her down. She's tired of me ranting about tenants and developers. Wants me out of her house and off her property. Says I should go live in one of my 'ugly rental units.'"

"And she's mad because you won't sell to Marissa?"

Oliver's eyes narrowed. "Marissa was just another vulture. Sandra hated her too, but at least Marissa had the cash Sandra wanted. If it weren't for me, Sandra probably would've sold the lavender farm to her years ago. But now, Marissa talks about a lower sales price and Sandra had counted on a higher price. See? Buy low. Sell high. Sandra wanted high. Marissa wanted to buy cheap, package a deal and sell it to the highest bidder."

The pieces clicked into place, and a chill ran down my spine. Sandra had a motive. But I still wasn't sure what it was or who she wanted dead – Marissa or Oliver.

A THOUGHT CREPT into my mind: if Sandra wanted Oliver to sell so badly, would she go so far as to make his life miserable to force his hand? And if Marissa's death somehow tied into this, did Sandra have a motive?

Oliver kept talking, oblivious to my swirling thoughts. "Sandra's all about her award-winning garden now. She's obsessed. Only likes tenants who keep up their yards, plant flowers, make things look nice. She's even hinted that she wasn't thrilled about me renting to you, since she wanted to sell the cabin and renters tend not to plant gardens since it's so dry and too much to take care of."

"Oh," I said, unsure whether to feel offended or amused. "Good to know."

"She's always been like that," Oliver continued, his tone turning bitter. "Wants everything perfect. Wants me to sell off the properties and 'simplify.' I'm not the simplifying type, Kat. These houses, this land—they mean something to me. I can't just hand them over to the highest bidder, no matter how much she nags."

"Sounds like a lot of tension between you two," I said carefully.

"You have no idea," Oliver muttered. Then, as if realizing he'd said too much, he straightened and forced a smile. "Anyway, enough about that. I just wanted to apologize again for the party. Hope you're settling in okay."

"Is that all it was?" I pressed, watching him carefully.

He hesitated for a fraction of a second, his eyes narrowing almost imperceptibly. "Pretty much," he said, but the casual tone had a brittle edge. "She was petty, you know? Petty and... desperate."

He smiled then, but it was the kind of smile that didn't reach his eyes. "Sandra always says I rant too much about this stuff," he said, his tone shifting as if he were trying to regain his composure. "She wishes I'd sell this place and let her live in peace. But if you're planning to stick around, Kat, I'd recommend getting on Sandra's good side. Maybe start a garden. She loves a good garden. And she needs some more friends."

"I'll keep that in mind," I said warily.

"Oh, and speaking of gardening," he added, his voice almost too casual, "I've got some new cotton gardening gloves I can drop off for you. Really nice ones. You'd like them."

The words hit me like a thunderclap. New gloves? Was he taunting me? My mind raced back to the party, to the mysterious gardening glove on the doorstep and its matching twin sticking out of Evie's pocket.

"Thanks, but I'm good on gloves," I said quickly. "But I am curious about one thing. What about the tenant who lived here before me? Why did he move?" I asked, changing the subject abruptly.

Something shifted in his demeanor. The friendly mask slipped, and for a split second, his expression turned dark, almost predatory. "What about him?" he asked, his voice low.

"Curious how long he was here and what happened to him?" I asked, trying to keep my tone neutral.

Oliver stepped closer, his eyes locking onto mine. "Let's just say he stopped paying rent. Total scammer," he began, his voice a dangerous whisper, "I know how to take care of people who cause trouble. Tenants, rivals... anyone who thinks they can mess with my livelihood."

Chills ran down my spine, but I forced myself to stay calm. "That's... quite the philosophy," I said, stepping backwards.

Studying Oliver, I couldn't tell if he emanated good or evil troll vibes—he seemed to exist in perpetual contention with the world around him. He spoke of tenants as if they were invaders. He grumbled about the lake houses as though they had wronged him personally. And when he glared, his small, beady eyes narrowed like he was calculating the exact amount of emotional toll he could charge you for existing in his proximity.

Before either of us could say more, a sudden commotion erupted behind Oliver. A blur of fur and tails came charging up the driveway—Koa trying to keep up with giant Great Dane Pepper's lopping gait, and... Squirt? Yes, ghost dog Squirt, who apparently hadn't gotten the memo about staying on the other side of the veil.

The trio barreled straight into the back of Oliver's legs,

He flew up and backwards, landing with a sickening thud that made me wince.

"Oliver!" I gasped, rushing forward.

He lay there completely unconscious, his arms splayed out as if martyred by the Hounds of the Baskervilles. Squirt seized the opportunity to lift his ghostly leg and pee on Oliver's khakis.

"Squirt!" I scolded, though reprimanding a ghost dog felt as pointless as yelling at the wind.

Koa looked like he might follow suit, but I shouted, "No!" and he backed off, wagging his tail sheepishly.

I knelt beside Oliver, looking for signs of blood under his head and checking to make sure he wasn't dead.

"Oliver, are you okay?"

No response. But no blood either. Good thing.

And of course, out for a daily walk, Ted and Claire appeared, apparently trailing their unleashed Pepper. Claire took one look at Oliver's unconscious form lying in my driveway and Squirt's squirrelly liquid trail darkening his khakis, noted his chest rising, breathing as if he was just taking a nap, and shook her head. "This neighborhood," she muttered. Turning to me she said, "What did you do?"

"Do? Me? Nothing!" I was stunned that she thought I must have pushed him or something.

Ted hastened his step towards me and troll in the dirt. "His he dead?"

"No honey, he's breathing," Claire responded. "And it looks like Pepper peed on him. What happened?"

"Gotta cell phone? Just call 911! Dogs knee capped him from behind."

She pulled out her phone and dialed 911, explaining our location and the situation as calmly as she could. By the time the ambulance arrived, Oliver was starting to come around, groaning and muttering something unintelligible, clearly concussed.

As the paramedics tended to him, a police officer

arrived at the same moment Brenda and Sam hustled over adding to the growing pack of humans and dogs.

"We heard the sirens!" Brenda exclaimed, clutching a small bottle of Perrier in one hand and, oddly, a half-eaten cookie in the other. She squinted at the scene, her eyes a little glassy. "What's going on? And... why is Squirt here?"

I glanced at Sam, but he just looked at Brenda and said, "You had the last of the peanut butter cookies, didn't you?"

Brenda waved him off. "It was only half. And its kicking in a little so I'm eating the other half. I'm fine."

While removing Oliver's jacket, one of the medics accidentally dislodged a small baggie that fell to the ground. It contained a handful of mushrooms—pale, delicate, and alarmingly familiar.

"Don't touch those!" Brenda warned, her voice sharp. "They're death angels. One bite could kill you."

The medic looked skeptical but used a pen to lift the baggie and flung it onto Oliver's jacket. "We'll have these tested," he said. "But how do you know what kind of mushrooms these are?" His stare penetrated Brenda.

"Well, everyone who forages around here knows what kind of shrooms are deadly and what kind are fun. I mean edible." She half-heartedly fake laughed to cover her discomfort.

Fortunately, the police officer did not overhear and stepping out of his car, walked down a short incline to join our group.

I'd forgotten to watch Koa and he suddenly trotted up all pleased with himself, tail held high and decided to add to the chaos. "What's that in your mouth Koa?" I bent down just as he dropped a tiny human-looking jawbone at the feet of a very stunned police officer then promptly lifted a leg and peed on his shoe.

. . .

SAM SIGHED and turned to the police officer, who was holding the tiny fragment of skull with a pair of gloves that looked comically too tight on his hands. "Uh, listen," Sam said carefully, "there's a perfectly reasonable explanation for this."

The officer raised an eyebrow. "I'd love to hear it."

"Where's Pepper?" Claire asked suddenly, scanning the scene.

As if on cue, Pepper sauntered up with an adult-sized skull clamped firmly in her massive jaws, making the grisly discovery look like a casual chew toy.

"Oh, for crying out loud," Ted muttered, rushing to grab Pepper's collar. "Drop it, girl."

Pepper, of course, refused, wagging her tail as if she'd just won a prize at a dog show.

"I've got this," Claire said, crouching down with a treat that magically appeared in hand. "Pepper, sit! Good girl. Now drop it."

Pepper, reluctantly, obeyed, releasing the skull into Claire's hands with an audible plop.

The officer stared at the scene, his jaw tightening. "Does this happen *a lot?*"

"Well," Sam said, clearing his throat, "it's not exactly an everyday occurrence, but, uh... it's not unheard of."

The officer sighed and muttered something about needing a raise.

"Well," Sam began, scratching the back of his neck, "there's an old pioneer graveyard up on the hillside. It's on my property. Over the years, the weather and, uh, critters have... well, they've unearthed some of the bones. The dogs like to, you know, find them."

Ted, who had been quietly taking it all in, shook his head and muttered, "Well, at least someone around here knows where the bodies are buried."

"Not helping, Ted," Claire said, nudging him with her elbow.

Brenda, still holding her cookie in the air like a prop cigarette in a one-woman play, stepped forward and added, "It's true. We always put the bones back! We're very respectful. I mean, it's not like we're building a mini-golf course up there or anything. We haven't built anything over it. Just want to preserve it for history."

The officer didn't look convinced. "You're telling me that this puppy"—he pointed at Koa, who was now sitting proudly, tail wagging—"and the giant dane just happened to find a family of skulls from a pioneer graveyard, and digging up skeletal remains and not reporting them is normal around here?"

"Completely normal," Brenda said, nodding earnestly. "Koa's just... a very enthusiastic archaeologist in training – way too young to report his findings."

"Blame it on the dog," I mumbled, trying to keep a straight face. "He is quite the detective."

"Just officer is fine. Not a detective yet." the cop responded oblivious to the fact I was referring to Koa.

"Whatever," Brenda said, biting into her cookie for emphasis.

Before I could press further, the paramedics hoisted Oliver onto the stretcher, and handed the jacket to the police officer saying something only the cop could hear about evidence - and the police officer turned his attention back to Brenda and asked about the mushrooms. Brenda, still in full "helpful neighbor" mode, warned them again not to touch them without gloves.

"Those are Death Angels," she said with authority to the police officer. "One bite could kill you. And if you don't believe me, Google it."

The officer sighed again and bagged the mushrooms and

the skulls as evidence. "We'll take a look at the graveyard and send these bones in for DNA testing and analysis" he said, glancing at Sam. "But if I find out you've been sitting on a bunch of unmarked graves without reporting them, there will be consequences. And don't leave town until this is cleared up."

Sam nodded, his jaw tight. "Understood."

As the ambulance pulled away, I glanced down at Koa, who was now sniffing around for his next "discovery."

"Well, buddy," I said, ruffling his fur, "you've outdone yourself today."

Ted, holding Pepper's leash firmly, chuckled. "How do find life in Legacy Lake?"

"I think I need a cookie or a G & T before I answer that."

14

DRIVEWAY DETECTIVES CATCH
A CLUE

It was another balmy evening, and Legacy Lake's most dubious driveway murder-sluething team had gathered for yet another round of "let's accuse our neighbors of murder," served with a side of fizzy beverages and a light drizzle of suspicion. Ted had dragged out a few folding chairs. Sam pulled out an old cooler and filled it with ice, seltzers, beer and a bottle of decent white wine that I knew by now wasn't the best from his wine cellar – but cheap and tasty enough for neighbors.

Koa, Pepper, and Squirt were busy reenacting a doggy version of *CSI* in the yard, gleefully digging up bits of who-knew-what while we humans lounged in the driveway, doing our best impression of a dysfunctional book club. Only instead of discussing novels, we were dissecting the murder—or maybe it was liver failure—of Marissa, the least-loved member of our lakeside community.

"Alright, let's start with the obvious," Claire declared, adjusting her T-shirt that was bunching up under sweaty hot summer night boobs, with one hand while reaching for her seltzer water. She had a way of starting sentences like a prosecutor delivering her opening arguments. "Evie's going to get arrested. It's just a matter of time."

Ted, her husband, raised a skeptical eyebrow. "You think the cops are going to show up at her house with a warrant? Based on what?"

Claire sat up straighter, ready to present Exhibit A. "Based on motive, means, and the fact that I saw her walking into Sandra's house the morning of the party while I was walking Pepper."

I was beginning to realize that dog owners spy on everyone in the neighborhood while under the guise of walking their dogs.

Brenda leaned forward, clearly more invested in her glass of Prosecco than the conversation but always game to stir the pot. "What was she doing there? Sandra doesn't seem like the type to invite random people over for coffee."

"She said she was picking up some new lavender blend spray," Claire replied, twirling her glass in her hand. "She was chipper—Evie, not Sandra—and she said she wanted the spray for her office to help her patients relax. She even laughed about it! Can you believe it? *Laughed*. Like she wasn't about to potentially murder someone hours later."

Sam chimed in, sounding a little off center, and I noticed that the Sauvignon Blanc he'd been nursing along wasn't his first. "You think she sprayed Marissa with lavender death oil and poisoned her through aromatherapy?"

"It's not as crazy as it sounds," Brenda said, raising a finger like she was delivering a TED Talk. "You can distill *anything*. Mushrooms, herbs, you name it. Sure, I've never heard of distilling Death Angel mushrooms into a relaxing mist, but technically, it's possible. You can even use dehydrated plants, mushrooms and berries in distillations. They still retain and even concentrate the nutrients and potency."

Everyone turned to stare at her.

"What?" she said defensively. "I prefer my mushrooms in chocolate, but essential oils get into your bloodstream faster than you'd think. If someone distilled mushrooms into an oil and spritzed it into the air? Watch out. You'd be as good as gone before you could say, 'What's that smell?'"

Ted shook his head, muttering, "This is why I stick to golf."

"Speaking of sticking it," Sam said, turning to Ted, "I still think Oliver's our guy. He had the mushrooms, the motive, and he flat-out admitted he wanted Marissa gone. You were there—you saw the whole meltdown."

"Sure," Ted said, waving his bottle of Kokanee beer. "But I don't know if he has the brains to pull off a mushroom-related murder. That feels more... calculated."

I decided to weigh in with what I learned about the gloves – possibly tainted with mushroom residue, possibly planted by Oliver but currently residing in Evie's shed. For a few minutes the group sat in silence.

Jessie, ever the voice of reason—or at least the voice of real estate gossip—spoke up. "I think it's too convenient to pin this on Evie or Oliver. If you ask me, there's someone else involved. Marissa had more enemies than a game we play on family night called *Betrayal at House on the Hill*—and with just as many secret plots and monsters lurking in the shadows."

"Who in this area doesn't think of a real estate developer as a monster?" Brenda quipped, earning a laugh from the group.

"Well," Jessie said, tilting her head down to stare at an incoming text, "In Marissa's case, it wasn't just clients. She ticked off brokers, other developers, shysters—name a corner of the real estate world, and she had enemies there. Half the people at the county clerk's office probably threw a party when they heard she was dead."

I listened quietly, sipping my drink and letting the gossip swirl around me. It wasn't that I didn't enjoy the drama—I did—but my mind was preoccupied with the bits and pieces of the puzzle that didn't quite fit.

Then my phone buzzed. It was Maggie.

"Hold on, guys," I said, stepping away to take the call.

"Kat," Maggie's voice crackled through the receiver, low and serious. "You're not going to believe this. Someone in Marissa's office went through her files and found something big."

"Big like what?"

"Like land-acquisition big. She was planning to acquire a massive tract of land that included Sandra's lavender farm. She was going to try to strong-arm Sandra into selling."

I blinked, suddenly understanding why Sandra might have a grudge—or worse, a motive. "Sandra? She never said a word about that."

"Apparently, someone tipped her off," Maggie continued. "And get this—Marissa had also turned Oliver in to the county for rental code violations. The kind of stuff that could cost him thousands to fix. It's like she was trying to burn them down."

By the time I hung up, my head was spinning. I relayed the news to the group, and Ted immediately connected the dots.

"That's easy," he said, leaning forward. "If Sandra knew Marissa was targeting her farm, and she wanted Oliver to sell his properties, she could've killed two birds with one mushroom. Get rid of Marissa and frame Oliver. Boom. Problem solved."

"Except Sandra doesn't seem like the murdering type," I said, though my voice wavered with uncertainty.

Ted shrugged. "You never know what people are capable of when money is involved. And from what I hear, Sandra doesn't have much of it. The lavender farm is more hobby than income, and if Oliver goes to jail, or dies, she gets everything."

Claire let out a low whistle. "That's cold. Brilliant, but cold."

As the group fell into thoughtful silence, Koa and Pepper trotted back over, each carrying a stick—or, in Koa's case, another disturbingly finger-like object.

"Not again," I muttered, prying the bone from his jaws.

The group burst into laughter, but I couldn't shake the feeling that we were still missing something. Sure, Sandra had a motive, and Oliver was shady as hell, but this case was far from solved.

Eying Sam and wondering how to start, I just blurted out. "I wanted to ask you about something, but I don't want to come off as nosy."

"Ah," Sam said, leaning back in his chair with a knowing smirk. "Whenever someone starts like that, they're about to get nosy. Go ahead."

"Okay, fair point. It's about the pioneer graveyard."

Sam's relaxed posture stiffened slightly, and he set his wineglass down on the armrest of the chair. "Thought you might bring that up," he said, his voice cautious. "What about it?"

"Well," I began carefully, "why were you trying to hide it? Brenda let it slip the other day, and I've seen how you get all squirrelly every time someone brings it up."

Sam exhaled through his nose, his shoulders sagging as if he'd been carrying this weight for too long. "I wasn't trying to hide it so much as... figure out what to do about it. It's complicated."

I tilted my head, encouraging him to continue.

"The land up the hill," he said, gesturing toward the slope behind his house, "I bought at a tax deed sale – paid the back taxes and still keep up the payments. Technically, it is mine. But it's not just pioneers buried there. There's also a Portuguese family from Hawaii. They came out here in the late 1960s, bought the land and raised a few cattle. That old apple orchard on the hill? That was theirs. Planted the trees to feed their cattle—and get an orchid going. A few of the trees are still growing wild, though they're mostly for the deer now. They rented a place in town and hoped to save enough money to build their dream house."

My eyebrows shot up. "Portuguese settlers? From Hawaii? I had no idea."

Sam nodded. "Yeah, not many folks do. They were part of the paniolo tradition—the Hawaiian cowboys. How they ended up here as orchardists is a long story. I got to know the guy before he passed. His name was Manuel Morais. We called him 'Manny'. His wife and child died years ago and Manny buried them in the pioneer graveyard – illegally I might add. Manny died of a broken heart not long after. And left enough money to cover the taxes for many years. Eventually, no heir stepped up and when the land came up at a tax deed sale, I bought it."

"That's fascinating." I was genuinely intrigued given my hunka hunka burning love visitor's Hawaiian ancestry and my own Portuguese lineage. "So, what's the dilemma? Why not just preserve the graveyard and leave it at that?"

Sam ran a hand through his graying hair, the lines on his face deepening. "Because preserving it isn't as simple as it sounds. If I formally donate the land for historical preservation, it opens a whole can of worms. The county could take over, start excavations, bring in historians and archeologists —and don't get me wrong, I respect the work they do, but it means losing control of my land. It could even end up in the hands of the historical society or, worse, some developer with a sweet-talking lawyer who finds a loophole."

"Like Marissa," I added.

"Like Marissa. She was definitely after it. Angry because I beat her to it. But I didn't kill her."

He paused, rubbing his jaw as if debating how much to say. "On the other hand, if I leave the land alone, I'm sitting on a property I can't touch without disturbing the graves. If I ever want to build up there—maybe for Brenda and me when we're too old to deal with stairs in this house—I need to know exactly where those bones are so I don't, you know, accidentally put a foundation over someone's great-grandpa."

I nodded slowly, starting to see his predicament. "So, the dogs..."

"Yeah," Sam admitted with a wry smile. "The dogs helped. Pepper, even Squirt—back when Squirt was alive. They'd dig around, and I'd check the spots they showed interest in. Found a few bones that way. Marked the areas as off-limits for any future building. I didn't want to risk disturbing anything sacred."

"That's... unorthodox. But kind of genius. Creepy, but genius."

Sam chuckled, the tension in his shoulders easing. "Yeah, Brenda calls it my 'canine archeology team.' They've done a good job so far. But, like I said, it's complicated. If word gets out about the graveyard, it could bring in a lot of unwanted attention. Developers, historians, even reporters. And with Marissa sniffing around trying to buy up land for her projects, I wasn't about to advertise that I've got an unmarked cemetery on my property."

Everyone sat still, listening to a story they all knew about – except for me – and realized the implications of what Sam was saying. "So Marissa knew about the land and the graveyard?"

Sam's jaw tightened. "She suspected. I don't think she knew for sure, but she was pushing hard to buy it. Kept offering more money, making big promises about how she'd 'honor the history of the area.'" He scoffed. "Yeah, right. She would've bulldozed those graves without a second thought if it meant putting in luxury vacation homes. Whatever history was tied to that land, it wouldn't have stopped her from developing it."

"Do you think she would've done it illegally? Aren't there rules about stopping developments if skeletal remains, particularly Native Americans, or pioneer graveyards are found? And aren't there rules about tax deed sales?"

"Absolutely," Sam said without hesitation. "She had the connections, the money, and the attitude to make it happen. And if she couldn't buy the land outright, she'd find another way to get it."

"But why? Why was she so desperate to get her hands on that land?"

Sam hesitated, his eyes narrowing as if weighing whether to say more. Finally, he sighed. "Because it's prime real estate. The lake view from up there is unbeatable. And it's not just about the houses—there's talk of rezoning the area for commercial use. A resort, maybe even a golf course. Big money."

I sat back, my head spinning. "So, she wasn't just after your land. She was after the whole area."

"Exactly," Sam said grimly. "And she didn't care who she stepped on to get it."

We all sat in silence for a moment, the weight of the conversation settling around us.

Finally, I broke the silence. "What are you thinking of doing with the land?"

Sam sighed. "Can't sell or build for a while now. The police are going to be digging around up there and already told me they were bringing in a forensic crew starting in a few days. This land will be tied up and unsellable and unbuildable for a long while and I'm good with that. I can wait."

I believed him. And I believed that he was an honorable man. I fully accepted his story as gospel truth. But, something still poked my BS detector and flipped on another light. It was the look of relief on Sam's face. Relief that the land was tied up? No one wanted their land tied up by outside entities. Why was he good with that?

Brenda refreshed her wine glass and reminded us we still haven't figured out who killed Marissa.

So, we started eliminating suspects on the list the way modern detectives, armed with elite scientific means, unveil the killer - by taking a vote – facilitated by Brenda of course.

"Everyone who believes Evie did it – say Ay," Brenda pretended to have an invisible checklist in her hand and crossed off an invisible Evie when the Neys won.

"Everyone who believes Sandra did it – same Ay or Ney". Split decision.

"And Oliver?" The Ays won.

"And Kat?"

"Wait a minute!" I half shouted, concerned she was serious.

"Relax Kat, you couldn't hurt a flea." Everyone laughed.

And I hoped, neither could anyone present.

15

HUNKA CHUNKA FIRE AND TRUTH

That night, I crawled into bed feeling more exhausted than I had in weeks. My brain was buzzing with everything Sam had told me about the pioneer graveyard, the Portuguese Hawaiian settlers, and Marissa's relentless push to acquire the land. Koa, blissfully unaware of the whirlwind of human drama, snuggled into the blue blanket at the foot of my bed, letting out a contented little sigh.

"Somebody's had a big day," I murmured, reaching down to scratch behind his ears. He wiggled slightly, but soon fell into the deep, twitchy dream sleep of a puppy who's living his best life.

I turned out the light and sank into the mattress, pulling the covers up to my chin. Sleep came quickly—too quickly—and before I knew it, I was no longer in my bed but standing on the misty edge of a wild, windswept tropical shore.

The air smelled of salt and rain, and the waves crashed against jagged black rocks, sending sprays of foam into the night. My heart thudded as I looked around, unsure of where I was or how I'd gotten there. And then, as if drawn by some unseen force, I turned and saw him.

My hunka cunka burning love messenger.

He stood a few feet away, bathed in that firey glow that seemed to radiate from the inside out. His skin was bronzed, his muscles carved with the kind of precision that made Michelangelo's David look like an effete young man. The palm trees swayed behind him as if bowing in reverence, and flickers of firelight reflected off his perfectly symmetrical face.

He wore nothing but a loincloth and a carved fishhook pendant that hung from a braided cord around his neck. His dark eyes locked onto mine, and for a moment, I forgot how to breathe.

"Are you going to stand there drooling, or do you want to hear what I have to say?" he asked, his deep voice rolling over me like thunder.

I snapped my mouth shut, feeling my cheeks flush. "Uh, yeah. Sorry. Go ahead. Messenger of the gods."

He raised an eyebrow. "Messenger of your ancestors."

"Right, right," I said, feeling ridiculous. "So... what's the message?"

He stepped closer, and I could feel the warmth radiating off him, like standing too close to a bonfire. He pointed down at my feet, where Koa now sat, looking up at him with a curious tilt of his head.

"Koa is not just a dog," the messenger said. "He is the embodiment of your kapuna, a digger of bones, a revealer of truths. He was sent to you for a reason."

In my half-awake state, I stared down at Koa, who blinked up at me with his big, innocent eyes.

The messenger continued. "Koa carries the spirit of your kapuna. His purpose is to guide you, to uncover what has been hidden so that an agreement can be reached, and the people can rest in peace."

"An agreement?" I asked, my mind spinning. "What kind of agreement?"

"The land," he said simply. "The land where your kapuna are buried. It is rightfully your land."

I frowned, trying to piece it together. "Are you saying the pioneer graveyard and the Portuguese family... I'm connected?"

He nodded. "But his bones, and the bones of his family, have been disturbed by time, by greed, by those who seek to profit from what was never theirs to take."

Taking a moment to let this sink in I surmised that I am related to the Portuguese man. Well, my father was Portuguese but I never heard of any family residing in Legacy Lake. And I wasn't sure if he was saying Koa was the reincarnated Portuguese man or what. "So what does Koa have to do with this?" I asked, looking down at the little furball who was now chewing on a piece of driftwood.

"Koa will show you," the messenger said, his voice steady and certain. "He has already begun. The bones he finds are not random. They are clues, pieces of a story that must be understood before peace can be restored."

I felt a shiver run down my spine. "So you're saying... Koa is leading me to the truth?"

"Yes," the messenger said. "Keep the bones."

Before I could ask what he meant by *keep the bones*, the waves crashed louder, the mist thickening around us until the world dissolved into a swirl of gold dust and fire.

I woke with a jolt, sitting upright in bed. The room was dark, but the moonlight streaming through the window cast a soft glow on the floor.

At the foot of the bed, Koa was curled into a ball, snoring softly. I reached down and ran a hand over his fur, feeling a strange warmth in my chest.

"Okay, little guy," I whispered. "I guess it's you and me. Let's figure this out."

Koa rolled onto his belly, and yawned before crawling up towards my hip, snuggling up to me, then settling back into sleep.

I lay back down, staring at the ceiling, my hand stroking his soft fur, my mind racing. The dream had felt so real, so vivid. And the messenger's words echoed in my mind like the slow cadence of a drum beating towards morning.

Follow Koa. Trust him. Claim the land. Manny. Something about the name Manny Morais. My dad had mentioned someone named Manny when I was a child. And our last names were almost identical – my father was a Morai. Add the letter 's' and you get the typical misspelling Americans inflict on immigrants.

I didn't know where this journey would take me, but one thing was clear: I couldn't ignore it. The bones, the graveyard, the land—it was all connected. And somehow, I was at the center of it.

Koa let out a soft bark in his sleep, and I smiled despite the weight on my shoulders.

"Well," I murmured, "at least you didn't kill Marissa."

Suddenly, I realized that I may even more of a suspect – or next on the hit list - if it turned out I owned Sam's land. The only ones I knew I could trust with this possibility – yes, I say possibility – because I do trust ghosts but not all the way – is Maggie and John, her real estate attorney hubby. And I desperately needed to visit them, next.

16

DEATH AND TAXES

Maggie and I were sprawled in Adirondack chairs on my dock, each of us holding a cold bottle of beer watching John winding up like a major league pitcher before launching a neon-green tennis ball into the lake.

"Go, go, go!" he called out.

Koa and Sunshine, Maggie's Portuguese Water Dog, exploded forward like furry torpedoes, launching themselves off the dock in perfect, synchronized belly flops. Koa, as usual, was about half a second behind, his little legs pumping furiously as he tried to keep up with Sunshine, who was a seasoned lake-diver and master of fetch.

Sunshine reached the ball first, clamping it between her teeth with a smugness only an experienced retriever could pull off. But instead of swimming straight back, she took a detour—right over Koa's head.

"Oh God," I muttered, sitting up. "She's drowning him again. Good thing he is wearing a life jacket"

Maggie spit out a mouthful of beer, shaking her head. "Sunny no!"

Koa was flailing wildly, his eyes bugging out as

116

Sunshine released him like an inflatable pool floatie scooting out of her way.

"She's trying to establish dominance. Or being jealous. Some dogs want to be only children and she needs to learn to play nice."

John watched from the dock, shaking his head. "You realize this is the third time she's done that today, right?"

Koa broke free from the proximity of Sunshine's tyranny and paddled to shore, shaking free of the momentary panic and panting for more, salivating after the ball. *Lets do it again!*

I leaned back in my chair, shaking my head. "Between the dogs trying to drown each other and the neighborhood murder mystery, my life has gotten *really* weird lately."

Maggie grinned. "Speaking of mysteries, you said you wanted to run something by John?"

I nodded and took a sip of beer, watched a couple kayaking past the dock smile at the dogs swimming after the tennis ball before launching into the story. "So, my neighbor Sam bought a parcel of land just up the hillside from me at a tax deed auction. It used to belong to a guy named Manuel 'Manny' Morais who passed away a couple of years ago. And I think—*think*—I might be related to him and might be heir to that land."

John tossed the ball again, watching the dogs launch themselves into the water before turning back to me. "How related?"

"Well, that's the thing—I don't know yet," I admitted. "His last name was Morais. My maiden name was Morai and my father was Portuguese. And I seem to recall my dad saying something once about a guy named Manny. I remember it because my mom was angry and said something about Manny being his only brother and sent me out to play while they had one of their discussions."

John furrowed his brows, his Ray-bans slipping down as he lowered his head and reached down to lift Koa by his lifejacket back onto the dock before Sunny could grab his tail. "That's... interesting but hardly definitive."

"Exactly. But with my antiques and oddities business, I've seen name changes and correlations a thousand times. Immigration records, census workers, legal documents—names get altered all the time. One bad handwriting day and a clerk drops an 's.'"

Maggie nodded, keeping an eye on Sunny to make sure she didn't swim over Koa again. But Koa finally got the message and had learned to stay behind her.

John rubbed his chin. "So, you think this Manny Morais might've been part of your family?"

"It's possible," I said. "And if he was—and I'm his closest living relative—do I have any legal claim to the land?"

John exhaled and took a sip of his beer. "Alright. Here's the deal."

Maggie snickered. "Oh boy. Lawyer mode engaged."

John ignored her and turned back to me. "First, tax deed sales happen when someone stops paying property taxes. The county seizes the land and auctions it off to recover the money. But—and this is key—before they do that, they have to notify any potential heirs."

I nodded. "Right. But what if they didn't?"

John leaned on the railing of the dock. "If they failed to notify you, that's a *big* problem. Legally, they're required to make a 'reasonable effort' to locate heirs—checking probate records, sending out notices, even publishing it in newspapers. If they didn't do that, you could challenge the sale. But first you need to establish that you are related and his only heir."

Maggie whistled. "That sounds expensive."

John scrunched up his face in mock annoyance. "About as expensive as buying beer for your husband every time she offers his free legal advice to friends."

Maggie rolled her eyes.

John laughed, repositioned his baseball cap and his Ray-bans and took another sip. "If Manny died without a will, his property should've gone to his next of kin under intestate succession laws. If you're his closest living relative, then yeah—you *should* have inherited it."

I sat forward. "So I *could* get it back?"

John tilted his head. "Maybe. First, we need proof you're related. Then, we'd have to see if the county followed proper procedures before the sale. And there's a time limit—most states only give you a certain window to challenge tax sales."

Maggie squinted at me. "How do you know about this land?"

I hesitated, knowing I couldn't confess that I got the intel from a ghost. "Sam said the land was part of an old settlement, including a more recent Portuguese-Hawaiian family that raised cattle and planted apple orchards. He told me about Manny and when he mentioned his last name – I just had an uncanny feeling that we are connected. And that maybe it's kind of fate that I am here. I feel like I should at least look into it."

John nodded. "Then step one is proving your connection. If you can find birth, death, or census records linking you to Manny, a will or even DNA correlation, you'd have a real case."

I groaned. "Good thing I am no stranger to research. Sounds like I have to do genealogy research *and* legal paperwork?"

Maggie grinned. "DNA test would help. You could get one through a Family Genealogy site and check out your lineage. It would take some work but you've got nothing to do in the next couple of weeks but raise a puppy."

John glanced at me, giving me a knowing look as if he knew what I knew. "If Manny passed away but the tax deed sale was years later, it suggests someone was still paying property taxes even after his wife and kid died, and that suggests someone else held title to the land or he didn't intend to abandon the land and set up a trust that paid taxes. We will need to see who was paying the bills. If it was Manny, that's a strong argument in your favor."

Maggie tapped her chin. "Wait, he was still paying the taxes?"

I nodded. "Yeah. Apparently, he put the money into an escrow account, hoping an heir would show up."

John straightened. "Okay, that's interesting. If he actively maintained ownership and tried to keep it for his heir, that makes your case even stronger."

Maggie grinned. "This just keeps getting juicier."

John laughed. "It does. But you still need to talk to Sam."

I groaned. "Yeah, that's going to be *fun*. 'Hey, Sam, I might be your long-lost neighbor's sole living heir *and* the rightful owner of that land you just bought—care for a beer?'"

Maggie lifted her chin towards the dogs and stated, "Beer helps everything."

John drained the last of his bottle and set it down on the dock, turning his focus to the dogs who were sitting down, fixated on him and panting for more. "Start with research. Find proof of your connection to Manny. If you have something solid, then we'll figure out the next steps."

John leaned back against the dock railing, tossing the ball again for the dogs before turning back to me. "One more thing—Sam *can't* actually build on that land right away. Not unless he wants to risk losing a lot of money."

I frowned. "Why not?"

"Well," John explained, "tax deed sales come with legal strings attached. Each state has a deadline for challenging tax sales based on improper notice. Some states give heirs up to *ten years* to contest a sale if the notice was defective, while others limit it to just one to three years. If the tax deed holder—Sam, in this case—hasn't filed a quiet title action to officially clear the title, then legally, you or another heir could still challenge the sale."

Maggie let out a low whistle. "So, if Sam tries to develop the land, he could be sinking money into something he doesn't technically *own* free and clear?"

"Exactly," John said. "That's why a lot of tax deed buyers sit on the land for a while, making sure no one contests it before making big investments."

A lightbulb went off in my head. *That's why Sam isn't in a hurry to do anything with that land.* He wasn't just being cautious—he *knew* there could be complications, and he wasn't about to throw money into a piece of property that might not be his for long. I took another sip of my beer, processing the implications.

I took a deep breath. "Okay. I guess I have some digging to do."

Maggie clinked her bottle against mine. "And here you thought only your antiques business would uncover old secrets."

"We are all the bearers of the secrets of our ancestors," I replied in my best old, wise sage voice.

I sighed and took a long sip of my beer, staring out at the lake as the last light of evening turned the water to liquid gold. John caught hold of Koa, removed the lifejacket, let Koa shake off the lake water and nudged him in my direction where he now lay sprawled on the dock by my feet, completely exhausted. Sunny lay down at Maggie's feet with a. contented sigh.

For a few moments, we all sat in companionable silence —well, as companionable as silence could be when your brain was a tornado of legal questions, lost relatives, and the sudden realization that I might actually own a chunk of land without knowing it.

"So, to review so I have my facts straight," I said, shifting in my chair to look John in the face. "If Manny really was my uncle and I was his closest living relative, I might have had a claim to his property—except no one knew because I was using my married name?"

"Exactly," John said, leaning forward, resting his elbows on his knees. "And because of that, the county didn't notify you before the tax deed sale. That could be grounds for challenging the sale, but we have to prove two things: one, that you're the rightful heir, and two, that the tax office failed in their due diligence to find you."

I exhaled and rubbed my temples. "So... how do we do that?"

"First step is confirming the DNA link," John said, ever the practical lawyer. "If Manny had been in the military after the 1990s, there's a good chance his DNA is on record. Or the police could get a DNA match off his bones. If we get a match, that's hard evidence you're his niece. I can handle all the legal paperwork—ordering the test, verifying your claim, even starting the process to challenge the tax deed sale if you want to go that route."

I studied him for a long moment, feeling a strange mix of gratitude and disbelief. "You'd do all that?"

John grinned. "Kat, I argue about property lines for a living. This is actually *interesting*. Besides, if Sam bought the land without knowing it should've been yours, he might be willing to work something out. But if we don't act fast, and he decides to build on it, things could get a lot more complicated."

"Yeah, we wouldn't want to interrupt Sam's potential plans to construct a luxury resort entertained by pioneer ghosts under the light of the full moon," I muttered. "Actually, I think the police have it tied up for a while as they verify the grave yard existed and isn't some serial killer's dump site. And Sam isn't one to build a resort."

John chuckled. "I'll draft the paperwork. You'll just need to sign off so I can act as your legal representative. That way, if anything surfaces—wills, hidden trusts, or even more bones—I'll handle it before the county or some developer tries to sweep it under the rug."

I nodded slowly, the weight of it settling in. "Alright, let's do it. I have a feeling this is just the beginning."

"Welcome to property law," John said, raising his beer in a toast. "Nothing is ever simple."

It was long after Maggie and John took Sunny home that the full weight of ugly possibilities settled in—like a sumo wrestler doing yoga on my skull, pressing my temples into a first-class, non-refundable headache. This land puzzle - what if Sam really thinks I murdered Marissa? This land-thing might just make me more of a neighborhood pariah if the driveway detective crew were to launch the gossip grenades. But then again, if Sam killed Marissa over this land, I could be the next one buried in the pioneer grave.

17

SPIT AND TELL

I'd never been one for spitting into tubes, but here I was, sitting at my kitchen table, hunched over a tiny vial of my own saliva like it contained the secrets of the universe. Which, apparently, it might.

The DNA test John ordered after our conversation about Manny Morais and the land he once owned, arrived the next day. It was pricier than I thought because I had to do a more comprehensive test analysis that included mtDNA (maternal lineage) testing and the company promised results in 48 hours. The more I thought about it, the more I had to know—was I actually related to the man whose land Sam had purchased at the tax deed auction? Was I unknowingly entangled in some kind of lost inheritance? Or worse, a murder mystery? I sealed the tube, stuck it in the prepaid envelope, and dropped it into the outgoing mail pile with a dramatic flourish.

"Now, we wait," I told Koa, who sat at my feet, staring up at me with his usual expression of profound canine wisdom. He sneezed in response and promptly trotted over to his bed, flopping down with a dramatic sigh.

But I wasn't waiting idly. While my genetic material

made its way to some lab to be analyzed by science wizards, I had work to do.

I pulled out my laptop and fired off an email to Maggie.

Subject: DNA, Bones, and Koa's Latest Investigation

Hey Maggie,

You are *not* going to believe this. I just heard from Claire that the police have sent some bones in for DNA testing—yes, including the *skull* that Koa and Pepper so helpfully dropped at my feet while the cops and EMTs were trying to scrape Oliver off my driveway. Can you even imagine the look on that poor officer's face when my dog trotted over like, "Hey, here's a little something I dug up for you"? I swear, if Koa were a human, he'd have a side gig on *CSI: Legacy Lake*.

Here's the kicker—what if the bones match *my* DNA?

I know it sounds crazy, but hear me out. I did some digging (metaphorically, unlike Koa) and found out that my father, Lucas Morais, had a brother named Manuel. Manny is the biological child of my grandfather but never mentioned – as if he was illegitimate. My grandfather was a straight off the boat immigrant from Portugal who first settled on Oahu then moved to California. Lucas stayed in California, but apparently, Manny moved to the Big Island of Hawaii and became a paniolo cowboy. A *Portuguese Hawaiian cowboy*. I mean, that alone is fascinating.

But it gets weirder and it apparently confirms

only some of what the locals have told me. Manny had a wife and a child, but both *died here in Legacy Lake*. Drowned, supposedly, though old records and Sam claim it was the flu. I don't know about you, but that sounds suspicious. What if it wasn't an accident? What if something—or someone—was behind it?

My father, as you know, died in a car accident about ten years ago, and as far as I know, I'm his only child and I have no one left in my family to confirm any blood feuds or falling out. I mean why was Manny not mentioned in our family? I always thought my dad was an only child up until my mom let it slip that my dad had a brother. If Manny had no other heirs, then I might be the last surviving Morais.

Which means...

If those bones belong to Manny, I'm *literally* related to the skeletons in Legacy Lake's closet.

I should probably be more freaked out about this, but honestly, I'm just intrigued. It feels like I've stumbled into a historical true crime mystery, and I *have to know* what happened.

Anyway, just wanted to give you the latest on Koa's ongoing forensic work. If this dog doesn't get an honorary detective badge by the end of this, I'm writing a strongly worded letter to the department.

Call me when you get a chance—I need your take on this before I spiral further down the rabbit hole.

-Kat

I HIT send and leaned back, staring at the screen.

This was insane, right? And yet, here I was, sitting in my kitchen, waiting for a DNA test that could prove I was related to a long-lost cowboy whose family had mysteriously died in the very town I now called home.

Koa let out a soft *woof* in his sleep, his paws twitching like he was digging up more clues in his dreams. I hated to disturb him but I was dying of thirst and wanted to pull out my VitaMix blend up a very berry smoothie and sit on the deck in the morning son before it got too hot to do anything but lounge on my paddle board in the lake.

Opening the freezer door, I was frustrated to see that I was low on my organic frozen berries. I'd have to supplement with that gross dried berry powder if I wanted to intensify the color and nutritional value. Dried berries. Something about dried berries. Something about Sandra's flower arrangement and dried red berries niggled at the edge of my consciousness. Koa let out a yelp as I stepped on his paw. Apparently awakening once he heard me rattling in the kitchen his little brain shouted FOOD! and dashed under my feet hoping for a handout. I jumped back, knocking the glass jar of powdered berry all over the floor, glass and pink powder scattered everywhere. Reaching behind me for a wet sponge, I remembered the sound of a crystal decanter breaking as I wiped up the mess only to see how red it looked when wet. The sound of glass breaking. Red prosecco. It was the red Prosecco. Chambord. Not just the Prosecco.

18

A WALK IN THE WOODS

I needed to clear my head and Koa needed to pee (as always) so we headed up the spur road to the main road and within a few blocks, veered off the road onto a network of trails that led into the forest.

Dried oak leaves rustled under our feet, and I could smell the baking scent of pine needles on the forest floor. A few hidden birds called to one another – warning of our intrusion. The late afternoon sun filtering through the canopy in streaks of white sun beams gave me both cool shade punctuated by moments of blindness. Koa trotted ahead of me, his nose to the ground, sniffing with the kind of focus only a puppy could muster. This walk had been meant to clear my head, but my mind was anything but clear. The deeper we wandered into the woods, the heavier my thoughts grew, filled with questions about my family and the horrible party, suspects like Oliver and Sandra, the mushrooms, and the strange puzzle that was Legacy Lake. Then speak of the devil...

As I rounded a bend in the path, I spotted Sandra up ahead, crouched near an old oak log. She looked so focused, her hands gently brushing aside leaves to inspect something on the ground, that for a moment, I hesitated to interrupt her. But Koa had no such reservations. He barked once, a happy, high-pitched sound, and bounded toward her.

Sandra glanced up, startled at first, but her expression softened when she saw Koa. "Well, hello there," she said, her voice warm as she reached out to pat his head. "What are you two doing out here?"

"Just walking," I said, stepping closer. "And you?"

"Just searching around to freshen up my flower arrangements." She gestured to the small wicker basket beside her, which contained a collection of plant stems, broad leaves, and other flora that enhanced her flower arrangements, filling them out and adding a palate of background colors and textures that made her cut flowers pop.

"I meant to tell you that your flower arrangements at the party were stunning. Now I know where you get your material..." I hesitated, unsure how to steer the conversation. "Do you grow your own flowers?"

She nodded, as she carefully cut a few more stems from a low growing broad-leafed plant. "Some I add fresh. Others I dehydrate. Those usually go into vases that I don't add water to."

"I noticed you have some lovely vases. One looked like it was Baccarat crystal!"

Sandra smiled. "It is. Gift from my mother for my wedding. But the wedding never happened. Long story. Old story. I'll tell you sometime."

"And the canapés at Oliver's party—did you make those as well? You are really talented."

Sandra looked at me sharply, her brow furrowing as if growing suspicious. "I did."

I shrugged, trying to sound casual. "Just curious. I don't like mushrooms but it seemed Marissa thought they were wonderful."

She didn't respond immediately, her fingers tracing the edge of the basket as though weighing her words. Finally, she said, "Poor Marissa. I made those the morning of the party from some Chanterelles I froze from last year's harvest and a bit of goat cheese. Maybe the last thing she ever ate."

I decided to let her in on the news. "Did you know the toxicology report found traces of the Destroying Angel mushrooms in her system?"

Sandra's face paled slightly, but she didn't look surprised. If anything, she looked... sad. "I didn't know. And if you are wondering what was in those canapés, I wouldn't use anything like that," she said softly. "I'd never touch something so dangerous, not intentionally."

"So, you've handled them before?" I pressed, keeping my tone light.

Her eyes flicked up to meet mine, and for a moment, there was something guarded in her expression. "I've come across them, yes. They grow around here, especially under certain trees. I learned about them from a foraging walk that Evie hosted for the community a few years back. About 20 people came along. Including your neighbors – Claire and Brenda. Even Oliver tagged along. Why I don't know. He usually sticks to the road when he takes his walk and have never shown an interest in my gardening or lavender farm. But I know better than to pick them. I wouldn't risk it."

"Do lots of Legacy Lakers know about this fatal mushroom?"

She nodded.

"What about the lavender spray Evie picked up from you before the party?" I asked. "Could that have been contaminated somehow?"

Sandra sighed, her shoulders slumping. "I don't know. I distilled that batch myself. It was pure lavender, nothing else but a little chamomile hydrosol added as an underlying scent and calming enhancer. But..." She paused, her gaze drifting to the forest around us. "There's something I haven't told anyone, not even Oliver."

I waited, sensing that she was about to reveal something important.

"Last fall, I was foraging up on the hill near the old apple trees," Sandra began, her voice dropping to a near whisper. "I found a patch of mushrooms growing there, beautiful but eerie. They were Destroying Angels—I recognized them immediately. I was about to leave them alone when I felt... something."

"Something?" I echoed, leaning in slightly.

She nodded, her eyes distant. "Like I was being watched. I looked up, and there was a man standing there, tall, thin and broad-shouldered, with skin like burnished bronze and dark, piercing eyes. Dressed like old 1960s era guy, super short, denim cut offs, hippie headband, flip flops and nothing else. And he spoke to me. Oddly. Like pidgin English."

"What did he say?" I asked, my heart pounding.

"He told me not to touch the mushrooms," Sandra said. "'These are not for you.' Then I was startled because a deer and her fawn started running up towards the man. I turned to see them as they came up from behind me and passed me so closely, I could almost touch them, which is odd because deer steer clear from danger when they run. And when I looked back to where the man stood, the man had disappeared, just like that. And so did the deer."

I stared at her, chills running down my spine. "You're saying you saw a ghost?"

Sandra hesitated, then gave a small, almost embarrassed nod. "I don't know what else to call it. He felt... otherworldly, but also very solid and real. Just talked funny."

The air between us seemed to thrum with tension as I processed her words.

"I didn't tell anyone because I knew I would sound crazy," Sandra continued. "But now, with everything that's happened... I can't stop wondering if he was trying to warn me not to eat them."

"He actually said 'these are not for you'?"

She nodded, perplexed. "Almost as if he were saving them...rather than warning me?"

"Sounds like a reserved garden patch. Do you think someone else could have harvested the mushrooms?" I asked. "Someone who didn't get the warning? And maybe wanted to poison someone?"

She frowned, her fingers tightening around the handle of her basket. "It's possible. Destroying Angels are deceptive. They look harmless, even edible, to the untrained eye. If someone didn't know what they were doing..."

Her voice trailed off, but the implication was clear. Someone had deliberately sought out the deadly mushrooms and did not receive a ghostly warning. This ghost was pretty choosey about who he let raid his poisonous mushroom patch. Almost as if he were in on Marissa's murder and had planned it all along.

Koa barked, breaking the heavy silence. He had wandered a few feet away and was pawing at the ground, his tail wagging with excitement.

"What's he found now?" Sandra asked with a faint smile.

I walked over to investigate, pulling Koa gently back. In the dirt, half-buried under leaves, was another bone—eerily humanoid.

Sandra's face turned ashen. "We should go," she said quickly, her voice tight.

"What is it?" I asked, but she was already turning away, clutching her basket like a shield.

"I can't explain it," she said over her shoulder, "but something about this place doesn't feel right. Be careful, Kat. There are things here—things buried—that don't want to stay hidden."

With that, she disappeared down the path, leaving me alone with Koa and the bone he had unearthed. I stared after her, my mind racing. Sandra's ghostly encounter, her knowledge of the Destroying Angels, and her connection to the lavender spray were pieces of a puzzle that was beginning to fall into place.

As I picked up the bone and slipped it into my bag, one thought echoed in my mind: Whatever truth was buried here, Koa and I were destined to dig it up—one way or another.

19

DEFINITELY NOT ASKING

The sun had just begun its slow descent over Legacy Lake, bathing the sky in warm hues of orange and pink. It was the perfect kind of evening for a driveway gathering—one of those impromptu neighborhood meetings that started with someone casually bringing out a lawn chair and ended with an entire circle of people deep in conversation, clutching various bottles of wine and beer.

Koa was sprawled out at my feet, thoroughly exhausted from an afternoon of chasing squirrels and sniffing suspicious-looking rocks. Ted and Claire had just arrived, Pepper prancing beside them like she owned the place, while Brenda and Sam had already settled in with their drinks. Jessie was running late, but she'd texted to say she'd bring more beer.

Ted, ever the bearer of dramatic updates, took a long sip of his beer and leaned forward, his voice dropping conspiratorially. "So, I played golf with Chief Taylor today."

That got everyone's attention.

"Let me guess," Brenda said, waving a hand. "You lost."

Ted narrowed his eyes at her. "Irrelevant. The man had news."

Sam, who had been fiddling with his bottle cap, stopped and glanced up. "Good news or bad news?"

"That depends," Ted said, pausing for dramatic effect before continuing. "The police got DNA results back from the bones. Turns out, the child's skull fragment matches Portuguese ancestry—specifically, Manny Morais. They verified it with his DNA from army records."

I sucked in a sharp breath, my fingers tightening around my wine glass. My heart pounded so loudly I was sure Koa could hear it.

"The larger skull they tested?" Ted went on. "Most likely his wife."

A collective silence settled over the group until Claire broke the tension.

"Well, I don't know about you all, but I've decided DNA stands for *Definitely Not Asking*. Because I don't need to know how many bodies are buried up the hill, who they are or when they died." She shot Ted a look that shouted, *why did you have to say anything?*

Jessie snorted. "Please, in your case, DNA stands for *Drinks Nightly, Always*."

Claire gasped in mock offense. "Excuse me, I am not a big drinker."

Jessie raised an eyebrow. "Claire, last week you drank out of a coffee mug that smelled like it was more than tea. And you totally are not a teetotaler as you pretend."

Claire shot back. "If you're going to start throwing accusations around, maybe I should remind everyone that in your case, DNA stands for *Definitely Need an Alibi*— because if this murder investigation drags on any longer, I'm pretty sure you're going to snap and take someone out."

Jessie grinned. "Only if Oliver comes over uninvited and I have to sit through another one of his long-winded speeches about 'the good ol' days.'"

Sam, watching the exchange, leaned over to Ted. "See? This is why we don't need cable."

Ted shook his head. "I have more intel. If you ladies are finished."

Every head swiveled his way.

"They carbon-dated the remains," Ted added, swirling his beer bottle absentmindedly. "No foul play, at least as far as Manny is concerned. He was buried in the local cemetery—cause of death, official records say heart attack." He exhaled, then muttered, "Or, you know... broken heart."

Sam nodded solemnly. "Broken heart mislabeled as a heart attack. Happens more than people think."

"Especially when you lose your whole family like that." Brenda looked down as if contemplating her own mortality, staring into her wine glass.

I cleared my throat, willing myself to say something normal, something that wouldn't betray the fact that my entire world had just shifted. "At least they got some answers."

Ted nodded, but his expression grew more serious. "That's not all."

He took another sip before setting his beer down with a thud.

"The police have officially reopened Marissa's case."

That got a surprise reaction. Claire nearly choked on her wine. Sam sat up straighter. Jessie, who had been lounging comfortably, suddenly looked very alert.

"Wait," Brenda said, blinking. "You mean—"

"It's officially a murder investigation," Ted confirmed. "The Death Angel mushroom findings sealed it. Someone poisoned her."

A collective murmur rippled through the group. I could feel the tension rising like steam off the lake.

Jessie let out a low whistle and handed another beer to

Sam before cracking one open for herself. "Well, that explains why I saw two detectives at the café today. Looked like they were having a very intense conversation over their lattes."

"What do you think this means for Evie?" Claire asked. "They have to be looking at her."

"Or Oliver," Sam added. "He had more motive than anyone."

My mind was spinning, but not just from Marissa. Manny. The DNA results. His connection to me.

I had told no one—not even Sam—that I had taken my own DNA test. If Manny Morais was my relative, that meant I wasn't just some newcomer to Legacy Lake. I had roots here, deep ones. Six-foot deep ones to be exact.

And yet, here I sat, surrounded by people who had no idea that I might very well be the last living Morais with claim to land they believe is theirs.

Brenda refilled her glass and sighed dramatically. "Why is it that every time we have a driveway gathering, we end up talking about murder?"

"Because we live in Legacy Lake," Claire said.

"Because we might have a killer in our midst," Sam added, not bothering to sugarcoat it.

"Because we're basically an unpaid, wine-fueled version of *Dateline*," Jessie said with a grin.

Everyone laughed, but I barely heard them.

I wrestled with the question gnawing at me—should I tell Sam about my connection to Manny?

My gut twisted as I imagined the reaction. Sam had already admitted that he'd kept the pioneer graveyard a secret to avoid legal complications. If he knew I might have *actual* legal claim to the land he bought, would he resent me? Would it make things awkward between us?

I took another sip of wine, forcing myself to breathe.

137

Maybe I didn't have to say anything yet. Maybe I could wait for my DNA results, get concrete proof before throwing around life-altering revelations.

Or maybe I was just too scared to say the words out loud.

As the evening wore on, the tension melted away into easy conversation again—talk of weekend plans, dog antics, and Sam trying to convince Ted that his golf swing was getting worse.

But I couldn't shake the feeling that something big was coming.

And when it did, there would be fireworks.

20

TRIFECTA!

The morning started with a phone call from John before I could even take that heavenly first sip of my ritual morning cuppa coffee – cold brew in summer – hot in winter. Without the initial *hello how are you* pleasantries, he just got straight to the point - "Buckle up, you won't believe this."

"Okay, first," John said, in his best courtroom voice, "your DNA results came in. And since Maggie let slip that the police had already confirmed Manny's DNA from military records, I went ahead and sent yours to the detectives. Just got off the phone with em. Just as you suspected, you are related."

I nearly choked. "Wait—what?"

"Relax," he said. "All this does is officially confirm what we already suspected. You have a legal connection to Manny, which means you have a rightful claim to anything that should have passed to his next of kin."

"Wow."

"Yeah. Wow." John paused to let it sink in.

"And this leads me to the second clue in your land case, which, I must say, is my personal favorite."

That's when John told me about the closet. No, not his personal closet—though I was now convinced he had some nerve-wracking skeletons of his own—but *the* closet at the county records office.

"So, my paralegal, Shona, has been getting real chummy with the county clerk," he explained. "The kind of chummy that involves too much coffee, a suspicious amount of baked goods, and—most importantly—convincing said clerk to spill some secrets about a certain *storage closet* where unprocessed documents go to die."

I grinned. "Sooo you're saying the county was forced to —wait for it—*come out of the closet?*"

"Exactly. And, wouldn't you know it, in the depths of that bureaucratic purgatory, Shonda found a paper trail leading straight to you."

It turned out that Manny had set up a trust—one that had been paying property taxes on the land for years. But when the money ran dry, the land went up for auction, and, crucially, no one had thought to notify me.

"Since you were using your married name," John continued, "and the trust was in your maiden name, you were conveniently overlooked. It wasn't even a conspiracy— just good old-fashioned incompetence."

I let that sink in. "So, Manny knew about me but I didn't know about him. That's so sad. I think I would have liked to know him. And you're saying if the county wasn't hoarding paperwork like a doomsday prepper, I might've never lost the land in the first place?"

"Bingo."

I took a deep breath. "Okay, what's the third clue?"

John sighed. "That would be Marissa."

I rubbed my temples. "Of course it is."

Turns out, before her untimely demise, Marissa had been desperately trying to get her hands on the tax deed.

She had filed multiple requests to purchase it, but—because fate has a sense of humor—she had missed several crucial deadlines due to either clerical delays, bad timing, or her own arrogance. But her name was *all over* the tax deed filings.

"She came close, but Sam beat her to it," John said. "She was *not* happy about that. She even made a few calls to push the county to reconsider, but rules are rules. And Marissa, for all her power moves, was still bound by them."

I let out a slow whistle. "So, if she had gotten her hands on it..."

"You would never be able to lay claim to the land," John finished. "She would have made sure of that."

The thought sent a chill through me. If Marissa had bought the tax deed, she would have immediately built on the land and eradicated all evidence of heirs in the county records. And after she died, I could have been seen as a suspect. But fortunately, I knew nothing about this and have John to back me up on this.

Although John couldn't see the look on my face, I grinned. "Wooooow! Thank you John! I think I need to take Koa out for a long happy dance walk."

"Talk later," John muttered knowing his voice was being drowned out by a very excited puppy yipping at my heels as we danced a yappy happy dance.

21

SLOSHED – UPPITY SLEUTHING

This was becoming a thing. Spontaneous suburban crime-solving, fueled by beer, wine, and an ongoing game "Who Killed Marissa" expressed during our spontaneous driveway detective parties.

Ted and Claire pulled up their lawn chairs, Brenda popped the cork on another bottle of bubbly, and Jessie arrived armed with a notepad like we were about to solve the Scooby-Doo mystery of the century.

We were deep into our second round of "Who Killed Marissa?" when a police cruiser rolled up, and a pair of officers stepped out, looking more resigned than concerned—probably because they were used to this neighborhood's brand of chaotic involvement.

That got everyone's attention. The chatter died down, and suddenly all eyes were on the officers.

"Evening," the lead officer said, rubbing the bridge of his nose like he already regretted being here. "Figured we'd find you all together."

Brenda wiggled her fingers at him. "Oh, come on over, Officer Moore, you'd love our little get-togethers. Want some champagne? Or I have a cookie if you prefer."

Officer Moore flashed her a rakish grin, and I swear, stood up a little straighter and flexed his arms like they had history together. "We're on duty."

"Your loss," she said, taking a sip.

I wondered if she meant that figuratively but it looked like Officer Moore could have been her loss and suspected a little history between them. Although Sam was a great looking man and devoted to her, Moore looked like Channing Tatum on the set of Fly Me to the Moon and I would let him fly me anywhere. Not realizing I was staring at him while I lusted away, his eyes bounced my way and he gave me a once over, then laughed when I felt the flush of blush or maybe a hot flash rising to the surface of my cheeks.

The second officer, a younger guy who had clearly drawn the short straw in being assigned to this case, cleared his throat. "Chief sent us to update you on some findings and ask you a few questions. Figured you'd hear about it one way or another." He looked at Ted, nodded, and added, "Congrats on that last game of golf."

Ted smiled wide. Thrilled that the news about him finally besting the Police Chief with an eagle – two strokes under par - in the last hole had gotten around the precinct.

"The graveyard on the hillside has been confirmed as a pioneer burial site," Officer Moore began. "Historical records and carbon dating back that up. However—"

He paused dramatically, which I suspected was mostly for effect, but I appreciated the effort.

"The bones of Manny Morais' wife and daughter weren't part of that graveyard. Those were buried separately by Manny himself."

Sam looked down at his hands, nodding slowly. "Yeah. He told me. Said he felt guilty for not saving them. And he wanted them to look over the lake they all loved, despite not being able to get a legal burial permit."

Brenda reached over and slid her hand into his, her usually mischievous expression melting into the depths of love they shared that obviously ran deeper than the ocean. Then she casually took another sip of her champagne.

"And Manny?" I asked.

Officer Moore glanced at me. "Buried in the VA cemetery in Oahu."

I took a deep breath, feeling something settle inside me. At least Manny had been properly laid to rest.

"Oh, and one more thing," the officer added, glancing at his notes. "Kat—your DNA test results state that you're a direct relative of Manny. It looks like he was your uncle."

Champagne shot out of Brenda's nose. "Holy crap, Kat!"

My head spun. I mean, I *knew* this was likely, but hearing it confirmed was something else entirely. The weight of it settled over me—this land, this history, all of it was *mine* in a way I hadn't expected.

Sam's head swiveled so fast I thought it might fly off his shoulders, then stared at me, clearly digesting what that meant. "So that means the land—"

"We'll figure it out," I assured him with a wave of my hand. "We'll talk later. We'll work something out."

Sam nodded, but his face was a mix of confusion and uncertainty as he turned his gaze back to Brenda seeking support.

No one else knew how to respond and wisely realized this business was solely between me and Sam. With my newfound heritage officially confirmed, I knew there would be questions – but later. Meanwhile, the group turned its attention back to its favorite pastime: implicating Oliver in Marissa's murder.

Brenda, never one to miss an opportunity to stir the pot, leaned forward dramatically. "Let's be real, boys in blue—

you want to ask us who we think killed Marissa and I think all signs point to Oliver."

Officer Moore sighed. "Brenda, this isn't a game of Clue."

"Oh, but it *is*," she insisted. "And I'm about to lay it all out for you."

She held up one finger. "One—he knew where to find the mushrooms."

Claire nodded. "Yep. Death Angels don't exactly grow in the produce section."

Brenda held up a second finger. "Two—he gave Marissa a canapé to try the morning she came to pick up hydrosols."

Jessie wrinkled her nose. "She *ate* something Oliver made?"

"Yeah, that's the real crime," Ted muttered.

Brenda continued. "Three—he had the gloves. And got sick after the party probably due to mushroom residue – you should check that out. *And* tried to pin it on Evie by planting them in her pocket."

Claire crossed her arms. "And four—he literally had the mushrooms on him when the EMTs worked on him in Kat's driveway."

Officer Moore sighed. "Which is circumstantial at best."

Sam, who had been quiet up until now, let out a slow exhale. "You're going to question him again, right? Maybe even get a search warrant?"

"We're working on it," the younger officer assured him.

Claire, however, wasn't convinced Oliver was the only suspect. "All signs *also* point to Evie," she argued. "She had the gloves, she was at Oliver's house the morning of the party, and she knows how to forage for poisonous plants."

Jessie shook her head. "It's too convenient. What if we're missing something?"

Ted sipped his beer. "I'm staying out of this one."

Brenda gave him a look. "Well, that's no fun."

Then Jessie piped up. "What about Sandra?"

Officer Moore rubbed his temples. "I don't suppose this conversation is leading to *less* work for us?"

Jessie ignored him. "Sandra had plenty of motive. Marissa was trying to push her out of her lavender farm and every other lakefront property she owned. It's not crazy to think she might've snapped."

I shifted in my seat. "I actually ran into Sandra in the woods recently. We talked for a while, and honestly? I really doubt she'd kill Marissa. She was rattled, but it didn't feel *guilty* rattled. More like 'I just saw a ghost and now I need a cup of tea' rattled."

Brenda lifted her champagne glass. "Ghosts are on brand for this neighborhood."

Deciding not to hold back, I turned my attention to the officer and filled him in on what else I noticed at the party. "You know, I was so rattled at the party that I just wanted to go home. But since then, I've remembered a few details about that night and discovered a few things in the past couple of weeks."

The officer leaned towards me, obviously interested – in the facts of the case, but I was beginning to hope he had a little interest in me personally. And so did the others – interested in the facts... but not interested in me in that way. Anyway...

"You know I brought the Prosecco to the party and initially people suspected that it was the bubbly that bubbled up from Marissa after she drank it. And I'll bet the MDs initially attributed the red, foamy stuff to blood coming out of her mouth was from her liver and the clutching her chest to the heart attack. But just before she collapsed, I remember Sandra pulling a crystal decanter out of a cupboard full of Chambord, a raspberry liqueur, that

Marissa liberally poured into her flute of prosecco, turning it a deep pink.

'Sandra also dehydrates plants and adds them to her flower arrangements. One of the arrangements I noticed in a rather expensive vase – I notice vases because I was... um...am dealing in antiques – held a mix of fresh flowers and stalks of dried lavender and Lily of the Valley berries. I believe if you check out her house, you will find evidence of Lily of the Valley plants and berries. The berries are known to be lethal even if dried and still retain some sweetness that could easily have been mixed into Chambord.

'Unfortunately, when Marissa collapsed, she knocked the decanter off the counter and it is in pieces. By now, it's at the dump. But if it isn't, you could maybe find a connection. It could be the vase holds some residue although by now she has dumped out the flowers. So look for an antique, silver vase that held the stalk of berries and lilys and see if you can get some toxic residue off that if you cannot find pieces of the crystal decanter. That's your connection."

"A connection where?" the officer asked looking up from his note pad.

"The toxicology report. Two toxins in Marissa's system – one was Destroying Angel that can bring on food poisoning symptoms hours after ingesting, then cause liver failure. And the other could have been derived from Lily of the Valley, which could cause cardiac arrest immediately."

The group stood stunned into silence.

"And you know this how, Ma'am?" the younger officer inquired.

"I read it in Evie's book about poisonous plants while I was wondering what to keep my dog from getting into. I have the book at home but since it's borrowed, you'll have to get your own copy."

"Uh oh. Here comes trouble," Sam murmured, as two blurs of fur tumbled into the driveway.

Squirt and Pepper came racing in at full speed, with Koa hot on their tails. The officers barely had time to step aside before the chaos unfolded.

Pepper, the Great Dane, *body-checked* an innocent lawn chair. Squirt, the ghost dog, weaved through legs like a canine torpedo, while Koa—bless his chaotic little soul—chose this exact moment to develop a fascination with law enforcement.

He skidded to a stop directly in front of the young officer, wagged his tail furiously, and then—true to Squirt's training, lifted a leg.

A stunned silence followed.

The officer looked down at his now urine-stained shoe in horror. "Yuck. If you weren't so cute, I'd kick you."

With all eyes on the younger officer, no one noticed Squirt lifting his leg over the shoe of the other cop. And poor Pepper chose that moment to lean in for a sniff of the guy's crotch.

Sam, for the first time in since he heard about his land not being his land after all, *smiled*. Not just smiled—he *grinned*. Because Squirt had left the pee trail. But Pepper, the scapegoat, was getting all the blame.

Claire tried to intervene. "Pepper is a very excitable dog—"

The officers both glared at her.

As the chaos settled, the officers took their notes and promised to follow up. Got in their cruiser and left – no doubt to stop off at their homes to change their socks before going back to work.

As for us, we poured another round of drinks and took stock of what we knew:

1. Oliver was looking *really* guilty.
2. Evie was still suspicious.
3. Sandra had a motive but probably no evidence remained.
4. Koa, Pepper and Squirt may or may not have just escalated tensions between canines and law enforcement.
5. After that free pee finale, I probably didn't stand a chance with Officer Moore.

FINALLY, dusk now faded from purple to black, we all started making excuses to leave. Brenda stood up and announced the next official meeting of the driveway detectives – as she had just nicknamed the group – would be two nights from now. And promised we would all hear Kat's story. I nodded. Tired. Gathered Koa into my arms and started for home.

A CHORUS of agreement followed as everyone started stacking their chairs into Sam's garage and Ted's garage next door. As we all headed to our respective houses, Ted called out, "So, two nights from now? Same place?"

EVERYONE LAUGHED. Where else would we be?

22

DRIVEWAY JUSTICE

The driveway sleuthing party was in full swing by the time Oliver crashed it, stomping up the road like a deranged postal worker on a caffeine bender. The rest of us were lounging in a semi-circle of lawn chairs, wine and beer flowing, theories flying, and Koa happily chewing on what I prayed was a stick.

"Oliver!" Claire called out in mock surprise as he trudged toward us, clutching what looked like a letter of doom. "What brings you here? Time for confession?"

"You despicable people," Oliver hissed, waving a sheaf of papers in the air like an enraged substitute teacher, "are ruining my life!"

"We've been called worse," Brenda quipped, topping off her glass of bubbly.

"This isn't a joke!" Oliver snapped, his face a mottled shade of red that suggested his blood pressure was on its own murderous rampage. "You've been accusing me and Sandra of murder! *Me!* I'm a respected member of this community! And this here!" he held up the envelope. "A warrant to search my house. Which they did.

"Respected?" Sam muttered, just loud enough for me to

hear. "You're like a Roomba that keeps bumping into walls and knocking over everything good."

Oliver wasn't listening. "You think you can just sit around gossiping and drinking, acting like you're Nancy Drew and her band of geriatric misfits—"

"Geriatric?!" Brenda squawked. "I'll have you know I am only 62 and can still do a yoga headstand!"

"Enough!" Oliver bellowed, his papers fluttering to the ground as he flung his arms wide. "I've had it with all of you! I cannot believe that you got Sandra arrested for Marissa's murder!"

Brenda, ever the opportunist, whipped out her phone and held it up like a microphone. "Go on, Oliver," she said sweetly. "Tell us all about it. By the way, I'm recording this."

Oliver froze, his eyes narrowing. "You're what?"

"I'm recording this," Brenda said, grinning. Brenda's thumb hit the record button so fast, it was like muscle memory.

"No, you're not!"

"Oh yes, she is," Sam said, pointing to the unmistakable red blinking light on her phone.

Oliver snorted, his lips curling into a sneer. "You think you're so clever? Fine. Fine! You want to know the truth?"

"Yes, please," Claire said, leaning forward like she was watching the finale of a reality TV show.

Oliver threw up his hands. "Okay, I'll tell you what I did!"

"Marissa," Oliver spat the name like it was poison, "was ruining everything! She wanted my houses, my tenants, my lake! And yes, I gave her that mushroom!"

The group collectively gasped, and someone—not saying it was me—might have spilled their drink.

"What mushrooms?" Claire asked innocently, though her eyes sparkled like a cat batting at a trapped mouse.

"The Death Angels!" Oliver shouted, pacing now, caught in his own tantrum. "I didn't mean for her to actually *die*! I thought she'd get sick, maybe back off, but noooo, Marissa had to make everything difficult, even her own demise!"

"Wow," Ted said – holding up his cell phone while on a call with someone. Two cell phones out of six recording. If we were younger, we'd have all whipped out our phones by now, live streaming it to the world.

"Oh, shut up, Ted!" Oliver snarled. "I did what I had to do! Sandra's been riding me to sell the lake houses, the lavender farm's bleeding us dry, and Marissa was about to steal my properties and turn them into a luxury condo resort! She pushed too far, and I pushed back!"

"Sounds pretty premeditated," Sam mused.

Oliver spun around, his eyes wild. "Don't you start with me, Sam! You've got your little pioneer graveyard, your fake moral high ground—"

"Fake moral high ground?" Brenda interrupted, her phone still aimed squarely at him. "This is gold. Keep going."

"Will you stop recording me?!"

Brenda lifted a corner of her lip into a smirk that kind of looked like a she wolf snarl ready to leap into the fray and protect her man. "You already said 'okay,' Oliver. I've got your consent."

"What?!" Oliver screeched, his voice cracking.

"You said, 'Okay, I'll tell you what I did,'" Claire reminded him, clearly enjoying herself.

"Which legally counts as consent to record," Ted added, sipping his drink like a smug legal eagle with one hand while holding the cell phone out in such a way I realized he wasn't using video, the whole deranged scene was on speaker phone for someone's amusement on the other end.

Oliver looked like he was about to combust. "That's entrapment! You're all conspiring against me!"

"Relax, Oliver," Jessie said, flipping her hair. "We're just your friendly neighborhood watchdogs. Think of us as the HOA of justice. Now just how did you get Marissa to eat a Death Angel?"

Oliver shook his head wildly as if stirring up scrabble tiles in hopes of a single intelligible word flying out and landing solidly on the board. Torn between keeping silent and offering up a full confession, Ted decided to nudge him in the right direction."

"Confession is good for the soul Oliver. You don't have to carry this with you," he intoned in his best priestly manner.

"Oh all right!" Oliver shouted maniacally. "I stuffed it in a canapé! Saw her at the house that morning trying to sweet talk Sandra into selling her lavender farm and I just snapped. I only tucked a little piece of it in the canapé-thing and thought she would get sick. Maybe I gave her too much. Oh God!" He started moaning.

Claire chimed in like a prosecutor seeking a full confession still holding the phone high and asked, "What about the gardening glove Oliver? Was that what you used to handle the Death Angel?"

"Of course. Of course. The glove. I dropped it when I ran away from the house after realizing that Marissa actually ate the mushroom and I got scared. I dropped it."

Claire pressed in with her line of questioning, "And Kat saw it on the driveway and put it on your porch bench the night of the party thinking it was yours. Then you stuffed it in Evie's jacket – both gloves – trying to frame her for Marissa's death."

"I didn't know what to do. Evie never used those kinds of gloves but my sister does. I would rather Evie take the fall than my sister. Blood is thicker than water and all that." He moaned again, this time collapsing onto his butt on the lawn and folding over forward, started rocking back and forth, humming in a weird high-pitched way – no doubt over the top with anxiety as he melted into a semi catatonic state.

The distant wail of a siren cut through the evening air growing closer.

"Well," Sam said, raising an eyebrow. "That was fast."

Oliver jerked his head up, looking genuinely panicked for the first time. "You called the cops?"

Ted shrugged, holding up his phone. "Was just on the phone with my golfing buddy – the chief of police – when you stormed up and started ranting. You've been on speaker phone."

Claire chimed in, "And I may have hit the button on Facebook for live video feed on the Legacy Lake page. You know, just for back up."

"You people are insane!" Oliver shrieked.

The siren grew louder, and moments later, a squad car pulled up to the end of the driveway. Officer Moore and Junior Cop stepped out, their expressions a mix of professionalism and mild amusement.

"Mr. Oliver Grayson?" one of them said, approaching with a pair of handcuffs in hand.

"What? No! This is all a mistake!" Oliver struggled to stand and both officers stepped in to help him, twisting his arms behind his back and reading him his rights.

"Doesn't sound like a mistake to me," Brenda chirped, playing the recording back for the officer with a Cheshire cat grin.

Oliver's jaw dropped, his face going from red to pale in record time. "You can't use that! I didn't mean it!"

"Tell it to the judge," junior cop said.

As they led him to the squad car, Squirt made a ghostly

appearance, lifted a phantom leg and let loose on Oliver's pant leg while Pepper ran up and stuffed her nose into junior officer's crotch as if obstructing an arrest, while Koa jumped up and down barking his excited baby bark, causing junior to step back while trying to stuff Oliver into the backseat of the patrol car. Officer Moore cracked a smile then turned towards me and said, "I'd like to call you and fill you in later."

"Looking forward to being filled in," I half whispered while nodding at the officer. Brenda caught it and stifled a laugh.

The officers drove off, leaving a stunned silence in their wake. Then, as if on cue, we all burst into nervous laughter.

"Well," Brenda said, raising her glass, "to truth at last and Sandra and Oliver's arrest! Well, maybe not Sandra. I liked her."

"To the truth finally coming out," Claire added, lifting hers as well.

And I added a toast of my own - "To unleashed dogs and friendships uncorked," I said, feeling a warmth—not just from the Prosecco but from the camaraderie of this weird, wonderful group.

As I grabbed hold of an overstimulated Koa and hugged him to myself to calm him down, I realized something: this might just be the craziest neighborhood I'd ever lived in. But it was also the first one that truly felt like home. Except now I wondered if I would be able to stay in this home. After all, my landlords just got arrested.

23

FIREWORKS

Sam and Brenda's house felt like stepping into a living scrapbook. Every wall, every shelf, every surface held remnants of a life well-lived—a framed photograph of Sam shaking hands with Jacques Cousteau, a shelf filled with old diving gear, and an entire wall dedicated to his underwater photography. Exotic fish, luminous jellyfish, playful seals, and even a few candid shots of Brenda in her younger years, free diving, effortlessly beautiful in the sun-streaked ocean.

Brenda, catching me admiring one of the photos, smiled. "That was back when I could still fit into a bikini without the risk of people getting seasick around me."

"Please," Sam scoffed. "You still look amazing. The only reason you don't wear bikinis now is because you think you're too old."

Brenda took a dramatic sip of her wine. "Exactly. Youth is wasted on the young."

I didn't know what she meant by that but I laughed anyway, the warmth of their easy banter made me ache just a little. Decades of shared memories, an entire home built together, filled with stories. Meanwhile, I had loved and lost a few times, married once, divorced once, and was just beginning to figure out who I am now as an older single woman and more importantly, where I fit in society. After the insanity of the last couple of weeks—the murder, the tax deed drama, Oliver being carted off in handcuffs—my sense of belonging felt about as sturdy as a sandcastle facing high tide.

Koa, oblivious to my existential crisis, was busy exploring. His tiny nose sniffed through every corner of the house, investigating all the strange new smells. Occasionally, he'd find something interesting and glance up at me as if to say, *Did you know they have dog treats here? And a whole bin of tennis balls? And the dog toy basket!!! I may never leave!*

Sam finally gestured for us to sit. "Alright, kiddo," he said, settling into his chair and rubbing his hands together. "Let's get down to business. What's are you thinking of doing?"

I pulled a manila envelope from my shoulder bag and handed it to him. "John, a real estate attorney who lives up on the ridge, had these drawn up. Basically, I have legal grounds to reclaim the land that Manny owned. Since he was my uncle, and the county didn't do their due diligence in notifying heirs, I can challenge the sale. If I win, I not only get the land back, but I can add to the suit that the county will have to refund you what you paid for the tax deed plus interest."

Sam opened the folder, flipping through the paperwork. His eyes narrowed slightly, absorbing the legal jargon. "And how long does this process take?"

"Months. Maybe a year," I admitted. "Government moves at the speed of an under-caffeinated snail."

He snorted. "Sounds about right."

"Or," I continued, "you could sign a quit claim deed, and I could just buy you out if you are willing to sell for what you paid for the tax deed plus interest. That way, you don't have to wait for the county to cut you a check. We could work out a fair price. And I'm sure John could work out an agreement with the county to reimburse me for the tax sale amount."

Brenda perked up. "So basically, Sam, you can get paid now, or you can sit around waiting for bureaucratic incompetence to come through. Because you know she has enough to prove legal ownership and government incompetence."

Sam sighed, rubbing his chin. "Manny would have wanted you to have it. He always talked about how much the land meant to him. He wanted to build a house, but life got in the way. It was never just property to him—it was home. He'd be happy to see family living there. And I would be happy knowing that as well."

I swallowed the lump forming in my throat. "I'd like to build a house," I said softly. "Something small, overlooking the lake."

Sam nodded. "That sounds right."

Brenda, ever the practical one, leaned forward. "Just promise us one thing—don't turn it into a glamping resort. We don't need a bunch of hippies setting up yurts and using our dock for skinny dipping."

I raised my hand solemnly. "No yurts. No resorts. No tourists meditating naked by the lake."

Brenda pointed at me. "And no telescope."

"Why would I—" I paused. "Oh."

Sam chuckled. "Yeah, our dock is for our own skinny dipping, thank you very much."

I made a face. "Okay, first of all, I now need a drink to erase that mental image. Secondly, no offense, but I don't think anyone over fifty is drawing much of an audience."

Brenda cackled. "You'd be surprised."

Sam sighed. "She's right. There's a whole niche market of people with bad vision and low standards."

I held up my hands. "I'm just going to pretend I never heard any of this."

The conversation shifted to lighter topics as we moved onto the deck and Brenda brought out a fabulous dinner of couscous, wild Alaska salmon, salad and her homemade sourdough rolls. Koa tottered from chair to chair hoping his cuteness would be enough to solicit bits of salmon not so discretely handed him under the table. The evening air was warm, carrying the scent of grilled burgers from a few houses down and from time to time, Koa lifted his head to catch the delicious scent. Out on the lake, boats bobbed gently on the water lit up by port and starboard lights – red and green. Brenda's string of lights surrounding their deck, reflected off the water below us like tiny fireflies.

The first burst of fireworks echoed across the lake, an early start to the Fourth of July celebrations, and Koa startled, yipped and ran in circles as the sky exploded. I reached down and drew him into myself, talking softly, calming his anxiety. Another burst and he lifted his head then looked at me, wondering how I was responding. "It's ok Koa," I whispered, holding him tighter. I plucked a tiny piece of salmon off the platter. And when the next burst of fireworks went off, I said, "Look!" and pointed at the sky where he following the colored lights falling into the water and lifted the salmon close to his mouth – a perfect pairing – fireworks mean treats! Nothing to fear here. And he settled into my lap, barely flinching when the next round of fireworks split the skies wide open.

Brenda popped open a fresh bottle of champagne, pouring generous amounts into our glasses. "A toast," she declared, lifting her flute.

"To what?" I asked.

"To new beginnings," she said simply, meeting my eyes with a knowing smile.

Sam raised his glass. "To not having to deal with Oliver anymore."

"And to Koa," Brenda added, scratching him behind the ears. "The best little bone-digging detective in the business."

"And to Squirt," I added, noticing the black lab suddenly appear next to Sam, his snout resting on Sam's knee as he looked adoringly into the man's eyes. Sam looked down at his knee and automatically reached down to pet Squirt, stroking his head and ruffling his ears.

I took a sip, letting the bubbles tickle my nose. For the first time in weeks, I felt something resembling peace.

Sure, there were still things to sort out—the land, the lawsuit, whatever secrets still lay buried (literally) around Legacy Lake. But for now, in this moment, surrounded by good people, faithful loving dogs that stay with us apparently for eternity, and a sky full of fireworks, I let myself relax.

Brenda nudged me. "So, next driveway party?"

I nodded. "Yep. I'll tell everyone the whole story about Manny."

"Good," she said, taking another sip. "Not to be insensitive but just so you know, if his wife and child's death wasn't accidental and it turns into another murder mystery, I'm going to need to bake a whole lot more cookies."

The End (for now)

Kat Morai and her Portuguese Water Dog, Koa, are finally settling into their new home above Legacy Lake—at least, that was the plan. But between construction headaches, nosy neighbors, and an ever-growing wine collection, things are already feeling *less* like a relaxing retreat and *more* like a sitcom waiting to happen.

Then a local viticulturist accuses Koa—and every other dog in the neighborhood—of slaughtering her chickens. Before Kat can clear her pup's name, she stumbles upon a body tangled in the vines. When a sinister note suggests she's next, it's clear that someone is more interested in *covering up* than uncovering the flavours of an excellent Pinot Noir.

With Koa's reputation on the line, her quirky, canine-loving neighbors jumping at the chance to play detective *again*, and a local ghost adding *her* two cents, Kat dives headfirst into another murder mystery. While they race to unmask the killer, Koa faces a "ballsy" challenge of his own—a looming appointment for neutering.

Fueled by Kat's wine cellar, the *Driveway Detective Party* team is back—armed with theories, charcuterie, and probably too much Pinot. As they peel back the layers of deception lurking among the vines, one thing becomes clear...

Legacy Lake isn't just a place to sip wine—it's a place where secrets refuse to stay buried.

After one too many blizzards in Legacy Lake, Kat Morai and her Portuguese Water Dog, Koa, trade snow for sand, heading to a beach house on Florida's Treasure Coast. Sun, surf, and an endless supply of Riesling sound like the perfect way to *not* find a dead body for once.

No such luck.

When the ghost of a shipwreck survivor appears, begging Kat to help recover the missing wing of her priceless antique gold bird and solve the mystery of her sea captain's suspicious death, things take a turn for the *paranormally bizarre*. But when someone starts sending Kat death threats, it's clear that someone—*living* this time—wants the past to stay buried.

Armed with her loyal (and overly enthusiastic) canine sidekick, a group of quirky treasure hunters, the local rock band "Stones Clones", and a supply of rum and Riesling, Kat dives headfirst into the mystery. But as she digs deeper into the legends and secrets of the Treasure Coast, she quickly realizes that X might not just mark the spot... it might mark her *grave*.

Can Kat solve the mystery before she ends up swimming with the fishes? Or will her tropical getaway turn into a *permanent* vacation?

A barkin' good read packed with mystery, mischief, and a splash of saltwater and spirits!

ABOUT THE AUTHOR

Hi,

I'm Julia Merlot. I live in the misty, coffee-fueled wonderland of the Pacific Northwest, where I divide my time between reality and the much more entertaining wonderland in my head.

I share my lakeside home with my muse, a Portuguese Water Dog named Koa, who keeps me on my toes (and off my chair, because apparently, it belongs to him).

Like my protagonist, I often daydream about owning a beach house—though unless I start selling books by the shipload, that dream will likely require at least three lifetimes. In the meantime, I graciously accept free accommodations in your beach house so I can write my next book. No, really. I pack light and my dog doesn't shed!

When I'm not plotting fictional crimes or avoiding Koa's side-eye, you can find me hanging out with my local driveway party sleuths and gossips, or in front of my computer plotting my next book.

Want to join the adventures? Please subscribe to my mailing list for book release give-aways and sneak peeks of upcoming books and series.

Shoot me an email!
katandkoa@gmail.com
JuliaMerlot.com

www.ingramcontent.com/pod-product-compliance
Lightning Source LLC
Chambersburg PA
CBHW041148250626

47164CB00015B/176